D E

'OK, Goldiloc

'Oh, no,' Mandy ̶ acute discomfort w ̶ myself into these m ̶

'I'm more interested in how you get out of them,' Brett commented drily.

'Mr Carpenter——'

'Don't you think you're being ridiculously formal given the fact you're in my bed? Not to mention that it would be more authentically Western if you used my first name.'

Dear Reader

Here we are once again at the end of the year...looking forward to Christmas and to the delightful surprises the new year holds. During the festivities, though, make sure you let Mills & Boon help you to enjoy a few precious hours of escape. For, with our latest selection of books, you can meet the men of your dreams and travel to faraway places—without leaving the comfort of your own fireside!

Till next month,

The Editor

Quinn Wilder is a journalism graduate who claims her training took something she loved and turned it into an 'ordinary old job'. In writing fiction, she rediscovered her passion for transforming blank stationery into a magical world she can disappear into for days at a time. Quinn likes camping, swimming in cold lakes on sizzling summer days, riding horses over open meadows, and swooping down mountains on skis. She lives in British Columbia's Okanagan Valley and finds it a peaceful setting in which to weave tales.

Recent titles by the same author:

BUILD A DREAM

DREAM
MAN

BY
QUINN WILDER

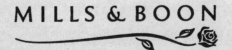

MILLS & BOON

MILLS & BOON LIMITED
ETON HOUSE, 18-24 PARADISE ROAD
RICHMOND, SURREY TW9 1SR

All the characters in this book have no existence outside the imagination of the Author, and have no relation whatsoever to anyone bearing the same name or names. They are not even distantly inspired by any individual known or unknown to the Author, and all the incidents are pure invention.

MILLS & BOON and the Rose Device
are trademarks of the publisher.

First published in Great Britain 1994
by Mills & Boon Limited

© Quinn Wilder 1994

Australian copyright 1994   Philippine copyright 1994
This edition 1994

ISBN 0 263 78774 5

Set in Times Roman 10 on 12 pt.
01-9412-48366 C

Made and printed in Great Britain

CHAPTER ONE

'HOME, home on the range,' Mandy warbled with determination, unpacking a pair of socks, a particularly favourite pair with polka-dot ruffles around the ankles, and putting them in the drawer of what looked to be an authentic antique bureau from the French Provincial era.

She sighed and stopped singing. It was no use. It didn't feel like home. It was never going to feel like home.

She bit back the temptation to put the treasured socks back in her battered suitcase, snap it shut, take it out to her car and drive away.

'Mandy Marlowe is not a quitter,' she admonished herself sternly, forcing herself to go back and rummage through her suitcases like a woman who had every intention of unpacking them.

'Home, home on the range,' she bellowed out, in defiance of the doubt that pestered her.

Her hand fell on a pair of scuffed and obviously very well-used binoculars. A grin of genuine delight passed over her small features, and her elfin charm became very evident.

She slipped the binoculars over her neck, gave them a little pat, and went over to her window. She flung back the curtains she had so firmly closed the minute she had entered the room, and looked out over the landscape.

The ranch house, if this Tudor-style monstrosity could be called that, was situated in a bowl surrounded by low, rolling hills covered in dry-looking grass. Wind had

forced it to be located at a low point in the land, which
Mandy found thoroughly disheartening because from a
higher place at least the Rocky Mountains could be seen
rising dramatically in the west.

From here one could see a few scraggly trees struggling against the ravages of the wind. A swimming-pool,
in a sad state of neglect, and looking as out of place
here as the house, was located directly under her window.

The land tugged on some lonely place inside her, which
was why she had closed the curtains.

Now she firmly lifted the binoculars to her eyes and
made herself sweep the surrounding landscape. Her room
was on the back of the house, and she noticed a cluster
of outbuildings down the road from her.

She trained her binoculars there, but saw nothing—
no, wait. A mangy-looking cat prowled across a
deserted-looking barnyard. She watched it until it slid
out of-sight under a fence. She swept the landscape once
more, and was about to put her treasured 'binos' away.
Maybe she'd try putting on her ruffled socks instead to
lift her sagging mood.

But just before she did turn from the window something caught her eye.

A small trail of dust was rising from the ridge over-
looking the ranch. She trained the binoculars on it, and
focused them.

She smiled. Now, that was more like it! A cowboy was
galloping a horse along the top of that ridge. She kept
the binoculars trained on him, as he came off the ridge
and surged down a steep incline into the bowl of the
ranch buildings. Kicking up a line of dust behind him,
he galloped the horse down a twisting trail towards
the outbuildings.

She watched, mesmerised. A dark cowboy hat was pulled low over his brow. His clothes were rugged and stained. There was nothing about him that suggested modern times or modern man. He might have ridden out of a different time in history. A time when life was harder and rougher, when men were required to be infinitely strong, resilient and independent.

There was a power in the man and his mount, a power that matched the lonely sweep of this landscape.

He belonged as she did not. He was a part of this world in a way she would never be, as forceful, as uncultivated, as unconstrained as the land itself.

The man brought the horse to a halt at a gate leading into the ranch yard, leaned over and opened the gate from horseback. Their pace easy now, the man and horse walked the final stretch of dusty road to the corrals.

Even from a distance, through the wavering sights of her binoculars, she could tell a great deal about him. His movement was the fluid, graceful movement of a powerful man. An outdoors man who wrestled the elements, and cattle... and probably a bear or two just to break after-lunch boredom.

His face was shadowed by the broad brim of a battered cowboy hat, stained from dirt, and rain and sun. A faded denim shirt, streaked with sweat and dust, was rolled up past the elbow of each arm. The golden tanned arms, corded with sleek muscle, confirmed that initial impression of strength, as did the broadness of his shoulders, and the depth of his chest.

Mandy felt happier already. That man was everything a cowboy was supposed to be and much more in keeping with her expectations of what to find on a ranch than this rather frilly, silly house.

Still very much unaware that binoculars were following his every move, the man swung down from the horse. His jeans, torn at one knee, and faded to nearly white, hung on narrow hips and hugged legs long and lean.

He turned and gave the animal an affectionate pat on the side of the cheek, and Mandy unashamedly studied the way the broadness of his shoulders narrowed to darn near nothing at the small of his back. She couldn't help but admire how snugly the worn-soft fabric of those jeans clung to his flat rear.

He loosened the saddle, and in an effortless motion that rippled every muscle in his arms, swung it from the horse's back and on to his shoulder. He disappeared inside the barn, but reappeared moments later. He removed the horse's bridle, put on a halter, then methodically he rubbed the animal down. Again his muscles corded and uncorded in a fascinating dance. Mandy found a little sigh escaped her when, with a final pat, he released the horse into the corral.

She smiled when the horse lay down and rolled happily in a brand of dust very similar to that which the cowboy had just so methodically removed. The man was leaning laconically against the post of the corral, and though his face was still shrouded in mystery because of the too-broad brim of that hat, she could have sworn he was amused, too.

He moved away from the horse, to a trough a few yards away from the corral.

He took off the hat. Mandy drew in her breath. His hair was jet-black, thick, with a bare hint of a wave in it. The colour was repeated in the dark slash of brows over eyes that glinted as green as the dark depths of an untamed forest. His features were regular and clean—high cheekbones, a straight nose, a faintly cleft chin.

'Lord,' Mandy whispered with appreciation. 'Can it get any better than that?'

It could—and it did.

Lean hands moved to buttons, and he had stripped off his sweat-stained shirt with astonishing speed.

Mandy's mood was improving by the second. She unabashedly trained her binoculars on the smooth, hard line of his chest. She shivered with awe. She had been given a calendar once for Christmas that featured bare-chested men that a woman absolutely drooled over—but she had never imagined such perfection could be *real*.

'Peeping Tomette,' she admonished herself, but with no real censure. Could she help it? It wasn't her fault that fascinating specimen had decided to practically strip in full view of her window.

The tall cowboy ducked his head into the trough. All of it. He pulled back out, and shook his head, the water scattering in a thousand drops around him, and his teeth flashing white in a sensual enjoyment of the cold water. The hint of a wave in that dark hair had turned into full-blown curls. He sluiced water on his arms, and then suddenly froze.

He straightened, and squinted, looking straight towards the house. Her window, to be precise.

There was something dangerous enough in that gaze to make Mandy hastily drop her binoculars from her eyes. Sure enough, the sun was at his back, and a tell-tale glint must have caught on the surface of her binos.

She waited a few seconds and then cautiously lifted the glasses back to her eyes.

That impossibly attractive cowboy had disappeared as though he never was, a dream produced by this immense and mysterious land that rose all around her.

She turned back to her room, and winced against the frilliness of it. It seemed even more a shock after the earthy rawness of the scene she had just witnessed.

It was a beautiful room. She knew that. The bed was beautiful, the furniture was beautiful, the pale pink and green pastel wallpaper was beautiful.

'I hate it,' she announced to herself, flopping down on the bed. She closed her eyes and her mind drifted home to British Columbia. To Anpetuwi. To her cosy little room with its homemade red-checked curtains and its rough log walls. To the view out of her cottage window—the sapphire blue of Okanagan Lake winking at her through the thick foliage of the trees. She felt a lump of loneliness rising in her throat. What had she done?

'Made a mistake,' she informed herself grimly. She forced her eyes open. She would not give into self-pity. It was not in her nature. Besides, it might not have been a mistake. It was really far too early to tell.

It was just that this place was so different from Anpetuwi Lodge, where she had been the entertainments director for the last four summers. In "real" life she was a kindergarten teacher, but she didn't find a great deal of difference between keeping adults and five-year-olds entertained. Still, whatever had possessed her to transfer her skills to a new location when she'd been so blessedly content with the old one?

'A man,' she reminded herself, with a rueful shake of her short dancing red curls.

She indulged in some more day dreaming. This time she was remembering her cousin, Charity Marlowe's, wedding to Matthew Blake. It had been a fairy-tale affair, held at Anpetuwi in the autumn. There was nothing more beautiful than Anpetuwi in the autumn, unless it was Anpetuwi in the autumn with a wedding in progress, Charity radiant in a long dress, of cream-colored ivory silk, Matthew more stunning than ever in that tailed black dinner-jacket.

The guest list had been international in flavour, given Matthew's involvement in the hotel business.

And one of the guests had been a stunning specimen of manhood, Lord James Snow-Pollington. Mandy, with her usual irreverence, had called him Lord Snow-Pea, and it had been the opening sally in a fun-filled week of having a man shower her with attention and spend all together too much money on her.

James, as she later started calling him, was tall and well-built, with burnished brown hair, a wonderful nose, and blue eyes that held as much irreverent laughter as her own.

He had to return to England, but in the next few months he called from overseas often, sent flowers, and notes and little treasures, and generally bowled Mandy right off her feet.

In the early spring he'd phoned and told her about his ranch in Alberta, a working cattle ranch of some size. He'd been contemplating turning the Big Bar L into a guest ranch, and would she consider taking on entertainment co-ordination there instead of returning to Anpetuwi as she generally did in the summer?

She shook her head morosely. She hadn't even stopped to think about it, which she was aware was one of her more glaring shortcomings. She had just said yes.

So here she sat, in the middle of a land so lonely it made her want to weep, in a monstrosity of a house that might have looked nice in the middle of the English countryside but which looked ridiculously out of place here.

And James hadn't said a word about whether he would be at the ranch this summer. His intentions, if he had any, were unproclaimed.

She forced herself off the bed, and caught a glimpse of herself in the gilded mirror above the dressing-table.

Her short, copper-coloured curls were in their normal disarray. Exhaustion from the long, gruelling drive had made her face more pale than usual. Her freckles stood out as if a wayward child had taken a felt pen to her face and randomly scattered dots across it. There were furrows in her normally smooth forehead and her large green eyes looked distinctly...frightened.

'Pooh,' she told herself firmly. 'It takes a little more than a few hundred miles of windswept nothingness to scare a Marlowe.' She crossed her eyes and stuck out her tongue at herself, and was rewarded when a little smile teased the edges of her mouth, revealing straight and gleaming white teeth.

Firmly, she turned back to her suitcase, and began flinging things into drawers.

'Boss, do you remember when I told you I thought Flame O'Hara was the most beautiful woman in the world?'

Brett Carpenter grunted. The boy talked a lot, but then he was just a boy. Only sixteen.

'Well, I was wrong. That's the most beautiful woman in the world.'

The words came out with such soft awe that Brett whirled from the horse he was looking at.

He narrowed his eyes. Coming down the road from the house was a woman.

And the kid was right. She bore a striking resemblance to Flame O'Hara, the country and western singing sensation, only she was better.

He watched her with narrowed eyes, waiting to see what the big sign on the fence post would do to her advance. The sign said "Absolutely No Guests Beyond This Point". When he had made the sign, he had just barely made himself refrain from adding "Violators Will Be Shot".

She glanced at the sign, and tossed her head so that those crazy copper-coloured curls caught the late evening sun. For a moment it looked as if she was crowned by fire. He heard the boy's gasp of astonished delight, and shot him a look of pure murder.

The boy didn't notice.

Who could blame him? She was wearing blue jeans that stretched becomingly over curves surprisingly voluptuous given that she was about as tall as fence-post. She had on a crisp white shirt that opened at the throat and gave an enticing glimpse of white skin speckled with freckles.

And those green eyes shone with pure devilment.

It would take more than a sign to keep this one out of his hair.

'Hi, there,' she said, coming to a halt in front of him. She shone a big grin at the kid, who nearly melted on the spot. And then she turned those huge jewel-green eyes on him.

She was thrusting a small hand at him.

'I'm Mandy Marlowe.'

Somehow the kid had squeezed right in front of him, and had taken that small white hand.

'I'm Blair Sinclair.'

The kid didn't look as if he had any intention of letting go of her hand, so Brett gave him a none too gentle tap on the shoulder. 'Go get that water, son. Now.'

The boy seemed like he had been startled out of a dream. 'Oh. Yessir.'

'I'll probably be seeing lots of you, Blair,' she called after him.

Brett felt a dislike for her leap in him. First, he wouldn't be at all surprised if it was this sexy little chit who'd had binoculars trained on him while he'd sluiced off in the trough after a hard, hot day.

Second, she'd ignored his sign, and third, she had that way about her. That way of a woman far too beautiful for her own good. And a woman who knew how to use that beauty to turn men into putty in her hands.

Slender hands, he noticed. Probably as soft as flower petals.

Still, he was no sixteen-year-old boy. He folded his arms over his chest.

'What can I do for you, ma'am?'

If she noticed that his voice was chillier than a January blizzard, it didn't seem to faze her.

She smiled, showing him straight white teeth, and just a flash of a little pink tongue. 'The first thing you can do for me is take down that awful sign.'

He *knew* he should have added the line about violators being shot.

'Take down the sign,' he echoed, aware of the temperature of his voice, already well below freezing, dropping a few more degrees.

She nodded vigorously, impervious to the cold, her curls bouncing around her head in a rather charming chaos that he tried to ignore. 'Yes, it will make people feel unwelcome.'

'Oh, darn,' he said. The blistering note of sarcasm should have warned her to hightail it to somewhere a whole heck of a lot warmer, but the woman didn't chill.

In fact, there was something about her that was red-hot, and it wasn't just that hair.

Maybe it was the lushness of those little bow-shaped lips as they curved into a beguiling smile.

'You don't understand. People who come to a guest-ranch want to be a part of it. They'll want to see the horses and sit around on the top pole of the corral cheering on the cowboys who are breaking the horses——'

'Maybe they could just watch with binoculars from their rooms.' He noted, with satisfaction, she was finally noticing it was a trifle chilly around here. The faintest pink surged up the dainty curve of her neck and into the delicate white of her face. Still, she wrinkled her pert nose charmingly at him, trying to melt him.

He refused to be charmed by her . . . or melted. He was a man used to wide spaces, and the brand of aloneness a man could find here like nowhere else in the world. He was a private man, and she was the type of woman who ignored "No Trespassing" signs.

'I'm not a specimen for you to study,' he said softly. 'I don't like being watched.'

The shade of pink had just darkened. A redhead's temperament, he decided, detecting traces of anger. So, she was going to fight ice with fire was she?

He didn't feel very threatened. Of course, he was not likely to be intimidated by someone whose face looked as if somebody had taken a paintbrush and splattered pale orange across it.

'Don't be so egotistical,' she admonished. 'I happened to be having a look at the landscape. You came into the picture.'

'*Egotistical*! I was practically having a bath. Pardon me for resenting a pair of unwanted eyes on me.'

'A bath,' she snorted. 'You had your shirt off. Are you Victorian?'

Egotistical and Victorian, he thought, eyeing her with distaste. His eyes caught on her lips, *again*. Her mouth was tiny, her lips red and sweet looking as fresh summer strawberries. A very unVictorian thought blasted through his brain. He was struck with the uncomfortable realisation that fire could do a lot of harm to ice, given time.

He turned away from her rapidly, bent and coaxed up one of Brandy's feet. He inspected it, hoping she would take the hint.

She didn't. 'About that offensive sign——'

He dropped the hoof and straightened. 'The offensive sign stays,' he said firmly.

'It doesn't,' she said just as firmly.

For a minute he was so shocked that if a gust of good old Southern Alberta wind would have come along it probably would have knocked him clean over.

'Who the hell are you?' he asked, not entirely sure if he was angry or amused.

'Mandy Marlowe,' she said, shoving her little chin toward the heavens. 'And who,' she hesitated, 'the hell are you?'

Amusement won. He almost laughed. She reminded him of a little kitten—all green eyes and bristling fur. But you didn't want to laugh around a woman like this. Next thing you knew she'd be giving guided tours of tired cowboys ducking their sweat streaked heads in horse troughs.

'I'm Brett Carpenter.'

'Oh, no,' she breathed, staring at him. He could have sworn those shoulders sagged momentarily, before she stiffened them. 'I'm the activities co-ordinator for the guest ranch. Lord Snow-Pollington said you would assist me in any way I needed.'

'He did, did he?'

'And for starters, I need that sign down.'

For starters. That worried him faintly, not that he'd ever let her see it.

'For starters, we need to set some ground rules. And rule number one is no guests beyond that point. And that includes you.'

Her hands had moved to her hips, and it was fighting stance if he'd ever seen one. Didn't she know it wasn't wise for a house kitten to take on a grizzly bear?

'I haven't got time,' he continued before any words emerged from her indignantly moving mouth, 'to baby-sit a bunch of city slickers who want a taste of ranch life but don't realise that could mean blood and broken teeth if they're in the wrong place at the wrong time. This is no place for tourists.'

'But it's a guest-ranch!'

'Actually, this is a working ranch, Miss Marlowe.'

'Ms,' she corrected him tersely.

'I should have known,' he said drily.

'And what do you mean, it's not a guest ranch?'

'See that offensive sign? Everything on the other side of that sign is a guest-ranch. Your territory. Do whatever you want over there. Bungee jump from the attic window for all I care. But everything on this side of the sign is mine.'

'But I can't run ranch programmes without access to horses! That's why people will come here.'

'Fine. That's why I hired Blair. He's young, but he's good with horses. He's going to pick out two dozen or so of the ranch's most even-tempered old nags, and he'll lead a trail ride once a day. Satisfied?'

'I most certainly am not! How can you be so unreasonable?'

'What's unreasonable about that?' He had felt as if it was a rather major concession to his absentee boss.

'I don't want trail rides. People will be dying of boredom!'

'Well, better of boredom than of a good kick to the head by a mean horse.' Or a mean cowboy, he added to himself.

'How on earth can I co-ordinate activities on a ranch if I don't have access to the ranch?'

'You look like the type that enjoys a challenge.'

'What type do I look like?' she demanded.

'You don't want to know.'

'Yes, I do.'

'OK, Ms Marlowe, you look like the spoiled, wilful type who knows how to manipulate to get your own way.

You look like trouble. In capital letters. But don't waste any of your charm on me, because I've seen plenty of trouble in my day, and I know how to handle it.'

'How can you say that? You don't know me from Adam.'

'That colour of hair is always a dead giveaway.'

'To what?'

'To the type of person who enjoys a challenge,' he said indolently. He hated to admit it, but he was rather enjoying riling her up. Those eyes were spitting sparks that could start wildfires if it were a touch drier out here than it was.

'Mr Carpenter, you are going to have to make some concessions.'

'I am, am I? Or what?' He watched her hands form fists that weren't much bigger than a good sized sparrow. He wouldn't have been surprised if she tried to sock him one.

'Or I'll have no option but to report you to your superior,' she sputtered.

He shrugged with infinite uncaring. 'You do whatever you think you have to do.'

She actually stamped her foot, which was about as big as a small gopher, and he couldn't stop the bubble of laughter that escaped him. He wouldn't be at all surprised if she tried to kick him in the shin.

'James owns this ranch! He can do whatever he wants with it.'

James, he registered. He wished the young lord would get to know a girl by taking her to a movie and buying her a pizza like everybody else in the world.

When he spoke his words were cool. 'That's right, he can. And he can fire me if he doesn't like the way I'm running my end of it, but he hasn't yet, and I have a sneaking suspicion he's not going to on your say so.'

He watched an interesting new development in her colouring. The pink in her face was actually starting to glow. Oddly, it made her hair look redder.

'Mr Carpenter, let's back up a few steps and be reasonable.'

He found himself liking her voice. She was trying to hide her huffiness but a funny little squeak in her tone—not to mention her flamboyant colouring—gave it away. But there was really no sense in his liking anything about her.

This latest idea, his employer's guest ranch brainwave, might last a week. Or it might even last the whole summer, but basically, in his mind, it was as doomed. Thank God.

'Look, Miss—I mean *Ms* Marlowe,' the gentle note in his voice even surprised him, 'The Big Bar L is not going to make it as a guest ranch.'

'I'm going to make it work, and you're going to help me.'

'Not on your life, Miss—Ms Marlowe. A trail-ride a day. That's the best I can do for you.'

He tried to harden his heart to her rapidly crumpling composure. Tears were gathering in the emerald of those eyes.

'Well, what do *you* want?' he finally asked, exasperated.

She sniffed back the tears. 'A rodeo.'

'A what?'

'And an overnight camp-out. Maybe a cattle drive.'

He felt his mouth drop open.

'And roping lessons. And do you think we could teach people to ride bucking horses?'

'Miss...Ms Marlowe——?'

'And campfires every night, and maybe a chuck wagon breakfast. And a barn dance.'

Her eyes had taken on a glow. He was a realistic man and he knew the reality of this guest ranch idea. He'd known it the moment that he'd got the latest letter from his boss. But he didn't have the energy or the inclination to try and explain it to her. She wasn't the type who took no for an answer easily.

Trouble, he reminded himself sternly.

'Look, put your ideas in writing,' he said with resignation. 'I'll have a look at them. I'm not making you any promises.'

In fact what he was really thinking was it would be easier to write a big black "no" across her proposal than to stand here all night trying to make her see sense. If he looked in those green eyes long enough he wasn't even sure he'd know what made sense any more.

'If you can find it in yourself,' he suggested wearily, 'try and be realistic.' He turned his back on the light of hope that had turned her eyes to a shade of green a man could drown in.

'Realistic?' she said. 'Oh, pooh.' She grinned at his glare, and turned and walked away. 'I'll have a proposal to you first thing in the morning, Mr Carpenter. Can I call you Brett? I don't really think we should have stuffy formality on a guest-ranch. It'll seem more authentically Western if we don't.'

What would that little chit know about authentically Western? I've created a monster, he thought. A green-eyed monster.

'You can call me Mandy.'

A green-eyed monster named Mandy.

She was walking away, and he dropped his eyes from the authentically Western way those jeans clung to her round little rear. Something close to her feet, near her ankles, caught his attention, and he narrowed his eyes.

He shook his head. Authentically Western. She was wearing the most ridiculous socks he'd ever seen in his life. Black polka dots and ruffles. On socks.

He shook his head again, as though trying to clear a bad vision. Well, he'd survived before, and he'd survive this summer, too.

At least, he was *almost* certain of that.

CHAPTER TWO

'HAROLD, that man had eyes so green a girl could practically drown in them,' Mandy informed the enormous teddy-bear that had taken up residence on her bed. 'Honestly, he was one handsome devil. Emphasis on the devil.'

She squinted into the trunk she was unpacking. Some time in the last hour, staying had become quite a bit more attractive a proposition.

'If there's one thing a Marlowe likes,' she muttered to the attentive bear, 'it's a challenge.'

She swung abruptly away from the trunk, scooped up the bear and sat him on her lap as if he were an overly plump child.

'Not that I have any romantic interest in him. I mean, he's just not my type. The furthest thing from it, actually. He's that serious, silent type. Not like James. James and I are kind of like two peas in a pod. From the 'life's a laugh' school of thought, you know?'

The bear had actually been a gift from James and she gave him a convincing squeeze. But it was not James's eyes that were haunting her. It was green eyes, clear and cold as jade. And it was not James's quick-to-grin mouth that kept creeping into her mind's eye. It was a mouth that was stern and yet undeniably sensual.

She was practically madly in love, for heaven's sake. With James. Did a man send you a teddy-bear like this if he didn't have serious intentions?

She got up restlessly. She liked James. She thought he was fun. And sexy. And intriguing. But she didn't know much about his world.

Or this one either. The thought of the brooding spaces outside her darkening window sent a shiver up and down her spine.

No, she had found her little niche in life. Though on the surface she could strike people as being zany and carefree, underneath her world was carefully structured and stable. She loved the sunny Okanagan Valley in British Columbia. She loved teaching kindergarten. This little adventure, her being here, at the request of a ridiculously wealthy English lord and at the hands of an enigmatic and altogether too handsome cowboy, were aberrations in a life she'd kept full of the familiar and the safe. She'd always imagined a cosy future, married to some solid and ordinary man.

A man like Gus. A funny little pain that she hadn't felt for a long time squeezed at her heart.

'What am I doing here?' she asked the teddy-bear imploringly. His glass eyes actually looked sympathetic.

'Doing what I do best,' she reminded herself firmly. 'Figuring out how to give *other* people the time of their lives.' She tossed the sympathetic bear heartlessly aside, and bounced to her feet. There was work to be done. In four days guests were booked to begin arriving at the Big Bar L. That left no time at all to indulge in self-pity over a decision made a long time ago. A wrong decision.

The opportunity to correct it was gone forever.

She rooted around through her desk until she found paper and a pen and then gazed at the wall.

'Try to be realistic,' she mimicked that arrogant up-
start of a cowboy. With a wicked grin and devilish flair
she wrote down bungee jumping.

'His own idea,' she said gleefully. On the line below
that she wrote mud wrestling. She chortled.

She had written both in jest, but it was like taking a
cork out of a bottle, and the ideas began to flow out
nearly as fast as she could write them down.

Hours later, she looked at her refined list, minus both
mud wrestling and bungee jumping, with satisfaction.

Tomorrow, Mr Brett Carpenter was going to have quite
an awakening. Tomorrow he was going to understand
that she was a professional, good at her job, to be taken
seriously.

She crawled into bed, exhausted and happy. The
darkness in the room was so complete, she couldn't even
see that awful pink canopy over her bed.

But she became aware of the lonely and restless howl
of the wind outside her window. Doubt pierced the ef-
fervescence of the bubble of confidence her high cre-
ative energy had formed.

How was she going to make others like it here when
she did not like it herself? That bleak and lonely landscape disturbed her, as did the constant sighs and cries
of a never-ending wind.

She groped around in the darkness for Harold, found
him, and clutched his furry, rotund body close. After a
long time she was able to shut out the lonesome song of
the wind, and sleep.

Mandy approached the corrals with a growing sense of
delight. She had worked late last night, and got up very
early in an effort to catch Brett Carpenter before he set

about his day's work, but now her exhaustion evaporated.

Now this was more like it! The scene could have come out of a Western movie. Horses and cowboys seemed to be everywhere. The men were dressed in faded jeans, scarred leather chaps, dusty cowboy hats, plaid shirts and denim jackets. Their deep, masculine voices blended with the snorts and snuffles of the animals and drifted on morning air that was mountain-fresh, faintly overlaid with the scents of horses and leather.

'One, two, three,' she counted the cowboys milling about, 'four, five, six...' There were nine of them. The number couldn't have been better.

A silence crept over their robust masculine chatter as she drew closer and they noticed her. She could see them shooting her sidelong glances as they suddenly, as a group, became engrossed in cinches and bridles, and tying bundles on behind their saddles.

She smiled to herself. Mandy liked men. She had grown up with brothers, and there was a fact about men that she was very certain of.

For the most part, they were scared to death of women.

'Good morning, fellas,' she called.

One or two of them nodded in her general direction. Two or three tipped their hats. One smiled shyly. A couple stared at her briefly before looking quickly away.

She stepped up to the closest man, and shoved her hand into his line of vision. 'I'm Mandy Marlowe,' she said.

With a slow, shy grin he engulfed her hand in his, and told her his name was Bud. She commented cheerfully on the endless blue of an early summer Alberta sky, and then went and introduced herself to the next man.

Ten minutes later Brett Carpenter came around the side of the barn. He looked quizzically at the horses, standing abandoned under the early morning sun.

He heard a shout of laughter, and his gaze went towards it. His men were standing in a happy cluster around...what? He squinted, and caught the briefest glimpse of a red curl emerging from that circle of men.

He folded his arms over his chest in utter disbelief. He watched for a moment longer, regarding each of his men thoughtfully. Not one of them had even realised he was here yet, so engrossed were they in that little puff of a peacock at their centre.

'OK, men, party's over. We've got a lot of work to do this morning.'

Startled looks were sent his way. Some of the guys actually looked sheepish. But mostly they didn't. They were backing away from her reluctantly.

'Bye, Mandy.'

'See you around, eh, Mandy?'

'Have a good day, Mandy.'

Brett could feel his back teeth grinding together so hard it was making his jaw ache. He purposely relaxed.

'Nice meetin' ya, Mandy.'

'We're gonna find you some real nice ponies for your trail-rides, Mandy.'

He became aware his hands were clenching and unclenching into fists at his sides. Deliberately he forced his hands open. Could these be the self-same men who had hung that sign with him, looking grim and determined?

'If y'all need anything, Miss Mandy, y'all just let us know.'

'Oh, I will,' she said sweetly.

She was standing alone now in the sunshine, her face flushed and happy from all the attention.

She was dressed in a pair of white jeans this morning, tight enough that he understood why his crew of hardened cowboys had just melted into marshmallows for her. She was wearing a bright yellow blouse, with delicate embroidery around the collar and the cuffs. It showed off her colouring and made her look as wholesome and sweet as fresh butter. He tried for a glimpse of her socks. If he was not mistaken, Tweetie-Pie was frolicking across her ankles.

'Ms Marlowe,' he said chillily, coming towards her.

'Good morning, Brett. We did decide on first names, didn't we?' Her voice was as bright as the sunshine.

'*We* haven't made any decisions, yet.' Damn her. Did she think she could manipulate everybody with that sunny nature and those glowing green eyes?

'It's a beautiful day, isn't it?'

'It's OK,' he said tersely. 'What can I do for you?'

'I brought down my proposals for activities for the guests. It's really neat that you have exactly nine guys working for you. Ten, including you, of course.'

He knew he shouldn't bite, but he did. 'What's so "neat" about it?'

'Baseball,' she informed him happily. 'Guests against cowboys.'

His jaw dropped. He stared at her incredulously. 'Are you out of your mind?'

'Just once a week or so,' she said hastily, eyeing his expression warily.

'My men are not going to play baseball to entertain your guests. My men are not toys who were put here for you and your fat, wealthy friends to play with.'

'You have a very negative attitude, Mr Carpenter.'

He was glad she was back to calling him Mr Carpenter. To him it signalled something of a retreat.

'I don't have a negative attitude,' he snarled. It satisfied him to see her back up a step from his tone. 'But I am not going to be walked all over by some half-pint redhead in a yellow shirt and silly socks. This is a ranch. It's been a ranch for more than a hundred years, and I'll be damned before I see you turn it into some kind of summer camp for adults with too much money and not enough sense to fill a thimble.'

Her face seemed suddenly very pale, her freckles dark against it. The hurt filled up her eyes turning them a shade of green he had never before seen—and hoped he would never see again.

'I don't think you have a right to judge me because of the kind of socks I wear,' she said bravely. 'And I don't think you have a right to judge other people because of the amount of money they have. People aren't coming here because they have a personal vendetta against you and your staff, Mr Carpenter. They are not going to be coming here with the express intent of making your life miserable.'

'I know that. My misery is just an unfortunate by-product of their dedication to hedonism.'

'It's not hedonism! The Big Bar L has been presented as a vacation option to these people. It's not their fault that you've decided you're above it all, and that some sort of law should be passed against having fun.'

'Just on this side of the fence,' he reminded her grimly. But she was fired up with passion now. Her cheeks had interesting red spots growing on them, her eyes were flashing and she was starting to jam one little finger in the direction of his chest.

He moved out of range of her finger.

'People aren't just coming here to have "fun", though there would be nothing wrong with that. They're coming here because they're tired, and stressed. They're coming here because they need to believe that somewhere a way of life still exists that is hard to find. They want to believe the great myth of the West is alive. That life can be simple and still invigorating, that people can be strong enough to live this lifestyle, and yet not lose the kindness and the caring that the West is legendary for.'

'Good lord, woman,' he muttered, moving away, again, from that stabbing finger, 'You should be writing speeches for the Prime Minister. Preferably the Prime Minister of a country far away from here. The Republic of Zaire, perhaps?'

She narrowed those green eyes accusingly at him. 'From what I've seen of your attitude, I guess it's a myth, anyway...that great strength can be tempered with great kindness, that there are places left in the world where caring about the earth and its inhabitants comes first.'

Fire and ice. That heat blazing down relentlessly until it melted all in its path, all in its way. He could hear the restless shuffling of the hands behind him, and knew the cowboys had been hanging on her every word.

'Hell, Miss Mandy, I'll play baseball once a week.'

Brett whirled and looked at Bud with amazement. Bud had voiced his objections to the guest ranch idea strenuously and in words that would have turned "Miss Mandy" into a quivering bowl of jelly.

'Sure, I will, too,' Mick said, giving Mandy a look so frankly adoring that Brett felt an odd desire to choke him.

'Ain't nuthin' much doing around here at night. You can count me in for a little ball.'

'Nuthin' wrong with having some fun.'

Mandy's colouring had been mysteriously restored. She was looking at him with a smile that put the sunshine to shame.

'I won't be playing any baseball,' he warned her in a low growl.

She shrugged. 'It would probably cut into your vinegar-drinking time. Here's the rest of my ideas.'

She was holding out a sheaf of papers that looked only slightly less thick than the Calgary phone book.

'I have work to do,' he snapped. 'You can leave those in my office. I'll get to them as soon as I can.'

'I thought we should go over them together.'

'You thought wrong.' There wasn't anything he wanted to do *together* with this little piece of dandelion fluff.

Unless it was kiss the living daylights out of her. He wasn't sure where that renegade thought had come from, but it made him even more certain that he wanted to get away from Mandy, the green-eyed monster, immediately if not sooner.

'You can leave——' he eyed the bundle distastefully '—your version of *War and Peace* in my office. It's at the back of my house.' He nodded curtly in the direction of the barn. 'That way.'

He turned away from her. Somebody had saddled Brandy for him, and the rest of the men were mounted. Gratefully, he went and swung up in the saddle, and led his men out of the yard.

It would have been a good exit—cool and dignified, except for the chorus of "Bye, Mandy"'s that followed behind him.

'Well, I never,' she muttered, narrowing her green eyes at him as he rode away. He might have ridden alone, the way her eyes singled him out, the way they focused only on him.

There was something about him that set him apart from the others. It was not the way he was dressed, for he looked rough and rugged this morning in working clothes of denim and flannel and leather. If anything, he had looked even tougher than most of his men, with a faint shadow of whiskers darkening that jaw, and shadowing the stony planes of his face. He looked more like an outlaw than the man running the show.

And yet the fact he was in charge was very evident in his carriage, and his command, if not in his appearance.

What was it that set him so irrevocably apart? The straightforward fact that he was the man of authority? Or was it that they were simple men, and he was not? There were definitely complications in the green gaze of Brett Carpenter's eyes. Complications that confused the way her heart worked. It started to scramble like a spooked bunny in his presence.

One thing was for certain: that man was not the least bit afraid of women.

Of course, it was probably pretty hard to be intimidated by a woman who had Tweetie-Pie on her socks.

She could not tell if she had won or lost round one. She was not certain how she knew it was a fight, with rounds to be won or lost, but she was certain of that.

With a deep sigh, she wandered around the barn. The dusty road twisted around it, and out of sight into a pretty little copse of trees.

'Trees,' she muttered. 'That's a nice change.' She followed the road into them, and felt a pang of homesickness. She liked the way light filtered through trees, green and tranquil. She liked the smell of trees, and the sounds that generated from them.

'Perhaps,' she muttered to herself, 'I can lead a guided tour of the one little grove of trees in about a hundred square miles.'

She stopped abruptly. A long, low ranch house was nestled in the trees. It was everything that the main house was not. A veranda stretched around it, and she could see the rough chimney of a rock fireplace.

'Now this is what a ranch house is supposed to look like,' she told herself. She grinned. 'Maybe I'll ask Brett if I can lead tours of his house. He'd probably like that. Fat, wealthy people poking through his things, and looking round-eyed at how a real cowboy lives.'

She was rather interested in how a real cowboy lived herself. He'd said the office was at the back of his house, but what better way to get to the back of his house than to go through it?

Feeling only faintly guilty, she went up to the front porch and tried the front door. It swung open easily under her hand.

She felt a shock of pure delight. The living-room was finished in aged wood, with a red tinge to it. The rock fireplace dominated it. Comfortable-looking furniture was grouped around the fireplace.

She walked briskly through the room, trying to maintain, even for herself, the tiniest illusion of being here on business. The kitchen was off to the left, and opened on to the living-room. Everything was gleaming with cleanliness.

She found the office easily. There was no missing it, no excuse to snoop through other rooms in search of it. She went in, and put her papers on a desk that showed the only signs of clutter she had seen in the whole house.

She noted, not without another small shaft of guilt, that there was a door leading directly outside from the office. She didn't take it. She went back into the hallway. Directly across from her was a bedroom. His bedroom?

'Mandy, don't,' she ordered herself.

Her feet, totally unheeding, moved over to the half-open door, and her hand gave it a shove.

The bedroom was beautiful in its utter masculinity. It had that same rough-hewn red wood. A big window looked out into the trees. A bearskin rug, black and shiny, lay on the gleaming hardwood floor.

A handmade quilt with some sort of native design had been tossed on the big four-poster bed.

She didn't even know why she did what she did next. It was just a mindless compulsion. She threw herself down in the very middle of his bed and felt a strange feeling of utter contentment as the softness of the bed welcomed her, and his scent enveloped her.

A beam of sunlight danced across her. She closed her eyes. Birds chirped happily outside the window. And, somehow, her eyes just didn't open again.

'OK, Goldilocks, wake up.'

Mandy started awake, and for a split-second was so disorientated that she couldn't remember where she was.

She sat up and gasped with shock. She was in Brett Carpenter's bedroom. And so was he!

She registered the anger in the stern set of his mouth, the flare of his nostrils, and the glitter in those devastating green eyes. She registered his scent—leather, horses, aftershave—and it seemed overbearingly masculine.

'Oh, no,' she moaned, trying to fight her acute discomfort with humour. She lay back down and threw an arm over her eyes. 'How do I get myself into these messes?'

'I'm more interested in how you get out of them,' he commented drily.

She risked a peep out from under her arm. Outside he was an intimidating man. Inside, his presence seemed to fill the confined space with a dangerously vibrating energy. The combination of his slitted eyes and his whisker-shadowed cheeks made him look more a renegade than ever.

'Mr Carpenter——'

'Don't you think you're being ridiculously formal given the fact that you're in my bed?' His voice was a purr of pure menace, and she risked another look at him and shivered.

'Mr Carpenter——'

'Not to mention that it would be more *authentically Western* if you used my first name.' There was a certain deadly satisfaction in the way he said that.

'Mr Carpenter, you're probably really angry right now.'

'Really?' he asked silkily.

'And you certainly have a right to be. This is inexcusable.'

'Inexcusable,' he agreed, that same hard note in his voice.

'And it will never happen again. I promise. Not in a million years.'

'Hmm.' She felt the bed sink underneath her, as his weight settled on it.

She sat up abruptly and tried to bounce off the other side, her heart scrambling wildly inside her chest.

A strong hand snared her wrist.

'You know, they never talk about what would have happened if those three bears had caught Goldilocks.'

'Let go of my wrist.' She did not think the smoky look that had invaded the green of his eyes boded well for her.

'Papa Bear might have taken it as an invitation, finding some sweet young thing in his bed.'

Her eyes flew to his lips. The faint smile on them was ruthless—ruthless and undeniably sensual. Her heart was beating a hard tattoo in her breast.

'Surely not with Mama Bear and Baby Bear looking on,' she protested, wriggling helplessly against the superior strength that was drawing her nearer to the iron wall of that chest.

'Mama Bear and Baby Bear seem to have gotten lost in the woods today,' he said huskily.

'You let go of me! You don't know the first thing about bears until you meet my boyfriend, Harold. He's very hairy and strong. And very jealous.'

'Is that a fact?' The hurting grip didn't release on her wrist.

'Brett! Let me go. You're hurting me.'

The grip on her wrist was released immediately.

'I won't sleep in your bed again,' she said with relief. 'Not without an invitation.'

Her relief was short-lived. The hand that had held her wrist moved behind her to the small of her back, and pressed.

She wedged her own hands between her chest and his, trying to fight the pressure that pushed her closer and closer to him. Her hands met the warm, hard surface, and lost strength. Lost will.

She let him pull her close, felt her breasts brush his chest. The pressure on her back lessened. She could have pulled away.

Could have, if she had not been held there, a prisoner of the warmth that was seeping through her, the unexpected delight that bubbled at the bottom of her belly.

She tilted her head up, and gazed at him, her eyes wide.

The texture of his smile had changed faintly. Knowing.

His lips touched hers. 'What kind of invitation would you like?' he asked huskily. 'This kind?'

He dropped his lips to hers. The kiss was as soft as butterfly wings touching a flower petal, completely at odds with the whiskers that scraped her chin, completely at odds with the faint mocking in his expression that she closed her eyes against.

There was nothing soft about the jolt that went to the bottom of her belly as his lips nibbled hers.

'I didn't mean it the way it sounded,' she mumbled.

His tongue, hot and silken, traced the line of her lips. 'How did you mean it?' he growled.

'I meant I wouldn't come in your house again unless you invited me.' The words came in reluctant gasps. Her brain didn't want to be bothered with words, with tasks like forming sentences. Her brain wanted to be put on hold so that her body could fully savour this—his lips touching her neck.

She wasn't thinking right. She wanted to not be thinking at all. Just feeling. Feeling tiny, exquisite pulses of energy leaping through her whole being, making her quiver and tremble against him.

'You know how to play men, don't you, Mandy?'

'No,' she protested. His tongue flicked in her ear, and it felt as if a firecracker went off in her tummy.

'No? You had those guys eating out of the palm of your hand this morning.'

'They liked me. I'm a nice person. Honest.'

'Nice girls don't fall asleep in strange men's beds.'

He was nuzzling her mouth, and sparks seemed to be igniting and dying within her breast.

'It was an accident.'

His mouth opened beneath hers, and with a sigh of surrender she sent her tongue into the warm invitation of it. Her hands curled around his shoulders, feeling the resilient strength of his skin beneath her fingers. She pressed more tightly against him, trying to erase any space between them, trying to feel fully the masculine energy that came off him in singeing waves.

Hard hands clamped down on her shoulders, and he put her away from him.

'Don't play with fire, Mandy Marlowe,' he warned her raggedly. 'You'll get burned. Or I will.'

She looked at him dazedly. At this precise moment in time she didn't want to be burned. That was an understatement. She wanted to be consumed by the fire that raged, red-hot, between them.

But the space he had created between them allowed the chill to creep in fast, to buffet her back to her senses.

He stood up, leaving her alone and shaken on the bed. She stared at him. His expression was closed and cold.

'Get up and get out,' he said tersely.

She scrambled off the bed, and turned her back to him while she tucked her rumpled blouse into her jeans. She felt dazed and disoriented, and dangerously close to tears.

'I don't want you to think I'm that kind of girl,' she whispered, not looking at him.

'What do you care what I think?'

'I'm not loose.'

'Look, Mandy, I don't exactly make it a habit of jumping into bed with strangers, myself. I'm not very proud of what just happened.'

'It wasn't your fault,' she admitted woefully. 'Brett, I'm sorry. I shouldn't have come into your bedroom.'

'You're right. You have a definite problem with boundaries.'

She sighed. Her fear—if that exhilarated beating of her heart could have passed for fear—was completely gone. 'I know,' she said humbly. 'I've been told before. My boss at Anpetuwi got really ticked off at me about it, too. He even confiscated my binoculars.'

She saw those firm lips twitch. She took it as a good sign. 'I'm not so bad. I'm just insatiably curious.'

'Snoopy,' Brett said unkindly.

She shook her head vehemently. 'No. Curious. Interested in people.'

'You came to be sleeping in my bed because you're interested in people?' He snorted.

'I just was having a tiny peek into your bedroom, because the house was so lovely and I wanted to see what a real cowboy's bedroom looked like, and there was this little sunbeam falling on the bed, and ever since I was a child I've loved to lie down in sunbeams——'

'Do you just keep talking until I give up?' he interrupted. 'Until I lie down on the floor and scream "uncle"?'

She regarded him thoughtfully, and her brow puckered. He was standing oddly, taking his full weight on his left leg. 'Something's wrong, isn't it? Why are you back here?'

'I had work to do here,' he said grimly.

'You're hurt,' she guessed suddenly, seeing that the lines of grimness in his face weren't all anger and exasperation.

'I'm not,' he said tersely.

'You are.'

'You're snooping again.'

'Well, you're lying!'

'So let's stand around in my bedroom and compare character defects,' he said drily.

'Do you need help?'

'God, no. I need you out of my bedroom is what I need.'

'I'll leave as soon as you tell me what happened.'

'You'll leave now or I'll kiss you again.'

That didn't strike her as being much of a deterrent, a feeling she didn't want to share with him, since it didn't seem it was reciprocated.

'You'd have to catch me first. And that would be hard, wouldn't it? It's your leg, isn't it?'

'OK, Miss Snoop, it's my leg. My knee, to be precise. Now would you go?'

'Could I get you some ice or something? I'd be glad to.'

'A little penance for your crimes? No, thanks. I just need some peace and quiet.'

'How did it happen?'

His sigh was one of long suffering. 'It's an old injury. I had an encounter with a Brahma bull several years ago. He won. Every now and then I twist my leg the wrong way doing something ridiculously simple like getting off my horse. Then I have to take a break from the saddle for a few days.'

'Were you a rodeo cowboy?' she asked with genuine awe.

'Once upon a time. Now, Mandy——'

'Our guests will be thrilled. A real rodeo cowboy. That means you *can* help me set up kind of a mini-rodeo.'

'I should have killed you while my hands were so close to your neck,' he muttered.

'But this is thrilling.'

'Would you get it through your little red head that I am not interested in being put on display for the entertainment of your guests? I am not for sale. My lifestyle is not for sale.'

'You misinterpret things.'

'No help from you, of course.'

'Well, there's a bright side to everything, Brett. If you're going to be laid up for a few days, you'll have time to look at my proposals.'

'Has anyone ever told you you're a menace?'

'As a matter of fact, yes.'

'Somehow——' he sank wearily on to the bed, and cradled his head in his hands '—I'm unsurprised.'

CHAPTER THREE

'THE last time I saw you, Ms Marlowe, it seems to me you swore you weren't coming back to my house without an invitation.'

Brett was leaning in his doorway, looking magnificent in a white cotton shirt and brand new jeans. His dark hair was curling damply, reminding her of the first time she'd seen him stick his head in that trough.

'In your house,' she corrected him. 'I swore I wouldn't come *in* your house without an invitation. Meanwhile, I have guests arriving in two days, Mr Carpenter. I need some answers.'

'Has anyone ever told you you're a pushy little thing?'

'As a matter of fact, yes.'

He stepped back from the door inviting her in, though she was certain she detected some reluctance in the gesture. She felt a trifle reluctant herself, given that their last episode together was not even twenty-four hours behind them yet.

'Don't worry,' he said softly, 'I don't bite.'

It was the other thing he did with that marvellous mouth that she was worried about, but she stepped inside his house.

She noticed his feet were bare. They looked nice against the polished wood of the floor. It was kind of homey catching him padding around in his bare feet.

'Do you want some coffee?' he asked, gesturing for her to have a seat in his living-room. He moved into the kitchen. He was still favouring his right leg ever so slightly.

Mandy noticed her proposal scattered all over the coffee-table. A masculine scrawl was visible in the margins. She craned her neck to see if she could get a preview of what he'd said.

'No, thanks.'

'Vinegar, perhaps?' he asked smoothly.

'Herb tea?' she countered.

A snort came from the kitchen.

'A glass of water would be fine.' She sank down in a plump chair, and let the deeply relaxing mood of the room creep into her bones. She'd been running on high anxiety since she had left here yesterday.

And not all of it had been caused by that deeply disturbing kiss on his bed.

'You look tired,' he commented, handing her a glass of water, and sinking into a chair across the coffee-table from her. He took a sip of his coffee and set it down. The rich aroma of it seemed well suited to his masculinity.

'Nothing is going right.' Probably he wasn't the wisest choice for a confidante, but he'd actually noticed she looked tired. He couldn't be quite as insensitive and brutish as he wanted to appear. He couldn't!

'No?' He raised an eyebrow at her.

There was something of an 'I told you so' in the gesture. It should have stopped her. This was not a sympathetic audience. But at least it was an audience of some sort. Harold's silent charm and sympathetic glass eyes could only go so far.

'The way things are going, our guests will unload from the minibus, and I'll say "Welcome to the Big Bore Lonely."'

Something tightened in his face.

'Don't take it personally.' How else would he take it? she chided herself. This was his home. He probably didn't even know there was a big, exciting world out there. This was his world. One hundred per cent.

'I won't take it personally,' he responded quietly. 'I can't be responsible for people being bored and lonely, though my experience with boredom and loneliness is that it's caused more by an attitude than an environment.'

That made her humbly admit maybe he knew more about the world than she initially thought. Quite likely more about it than she did.

'But aren't there any tourist attractions around here? A place where I can plan a day trip?'

'Nope.'

'There's got to be something.'

'There's the Frank slide. It's about an hour and a half from here. In 1903 Turtle Mountain came down and crushed a whole town underneath it. Would that do?'

'That's not exactly something to plan a day of light-hearted fun around!'

'Well, you asked what's around here, and that's it. I'm not an expert on frivolity.'

She sighed. He didn't even approve of frivolity, from what she had seen. 'The pool maintenance company doesn't want to come out this far to repair the pool.'

'Yeah, I know.'

'Well, why on earth didn't you tell me?'

'You didn't ask.'

'You're not going to make anything easy for me, are you?'

'No.'

'Well, why not? I thought you Western folk were always helping each other out.'

'When help is needed, we "Western folk" are there, all right. Sometimes it's more important for people to learn to do things themselves.'

'Meaning what?'

He shrugged with careless eloquence. 'Maybe you've had things too easy for too long. There's more to life than fluttering your eyelashes at people to get them to jump through hoops for you.'

'I don't do that.'

He levelled a look so long and hard at her that she blushed.

'I don't always do that,' she amended. 'Why do you have to turn everything into a war? What's the virtue in making things hard instead of easy?'

'Life out here isn't always easy. Besides, you're not exactly making things easy for me, either.'

'In what way?' she demanded indignantly.

'I've been taking a ribbing from my men about when you and I are getting married.'

For once Mandy was so shocked she couldn't speak.

'Did you have to go down to the corrals and tell them you were waiting for me to answer to your proposal?'

'I didn't mean that kind of proposal!'

'They'll jump on any opportunity to tease a dyed-in-the-wool bachelor like me.'

She regarded him thoughtfully. His cool green gaze had drifted out the window. He looked relaxed in his own home—and so attractive and sexy that it nearly set her teeth on edge. What a waste. He could be her dream man—if he never opened his mouth. If he just sat there like a figure from some hopelessly romantic Western movie, and kept his supreme arrogance to himself.

'Why are you a bachelor?' she blurted out.

He shrugged. 'This is lonely country. The girls stay around here until they've finished school. Then they either get married or move on. There's not much to keep a woman in this country. I wasn't ready to get married right out of high school.' He grinned, but the grin seemed to be masking something. 'But I'm ready now. I told the guys you and I were getting hitched in September.'

'You what?' she gasped, and then she laughed. So there was a sense of humour lurking in the moody depths of those green eyes.

'There's only one way to shut up a cowboy and that's to beat him at his own game. If I'd have got mad or embarrassed, I never would have heard the end of it. Now it's over before it got started, but in the future you might want to watch how you word things.'

'Hah. And make things *easy* for you? Not on your life.'

'I suspected not,' he said with a wry shake of his head. He took a long draw of his coffee. The humour was glinting in his eyes again, like sun glinting off a deep green pond. It made him seem almost human.

'Besides,' she said tentatively, 'I'm not sure if there's going to be a future.'

He made a small effort to look suitably sympathetic, but she couldn't miss the tug of satisfaction around his stern mouth.

'The chef quit. We haven't even opened yet!'

'Why?'

'Because he can't get fresh produce every day, and because the meat has to be frozen. Can you believe that?

I tried to talk him into staying but he seemed to be immune to my charms.'

'That must have shocked the hell out of you,' Brett commented drily. 'Two men on the same ranch that you can't manipulate.'

'I am not *that* manipulative,' she protested.

'Tell it to somebody who didn't see you wrap nine cowboys around your finger in nine seconds. If manipulation was a rodeo event, you'd have a buckle bigger than this one.'

She looked at the impressive silver buckle on his belt. 'What did you win that for?'

'Vinegar drinking.'

'Do you ever forget anything?'

'No.' For a moment his eyes darkened and settled on her lips. For a moment yesterday's kiss hung in the air between them like the ghostly scent of perfume.

'I need a cook,' she said hastily. 'Who cooks for you and your men? I'm sure you would have drawn and quartered him by now if he didn't provide good food.'

'Croc. Yeah, he's pretty fair with the grub.'

'Croc? What kind of name is that?'

'Short for Crocodile. Fair with grub, but crossed with a crocodile when it comes to temperament.'

'Do you think he might consider cooking for us, as well? Until we replace Pierre? We don't have a full booking for the first week. It would only be an extra thirteen people.'

'*Only*. If you were having company for dinner and somebody brought thirteen extra friends, would that be *only* to you?'

'Well, no.'

'That's what I mean by manipulation.'

'Some people would call it salesmanship.'

'Some people buy bridges, too.'

'Besides, I'm sure thirteen people is nothing to a professional cook.'

'I'm not sure that Croc is a professional cook. We're talking about a man who insists on putting a cigar ash in his chilli con carne.'

'Chilli! That's more like it. I didn't think gourmet French dining was in keeping with a ranch theme, anyway.'

'What about the cigar ash?'

'I don't care if he makes it with rattlesnakes as long as it tastes good. Can I talk to him? Do you mind?'

'It's a free world.' Brett sounded distinctly amused, as if he'd rather enjoy seeing her meeting with the man-eating Croc. 'Isn't there some sort of resort manager who should be looking after stuff like this? I met him briefly. What was his name?'

'Felix,' she said woefully. 'If I left it up to him, I don't think the resort would ever open.'

'There's a thought,' Brett muttered. 'What exactly is wrong with Felix?'

'I think he's a tippler. He's not very organised. He just walks around wringing his hands and complaining. Then he disappears and comes back smelling like strong aftershave. At least then he stops wringing his hands.'

'Do you have a lock on your bedroom door?' Brett asked casually. Too casually.

'Yes, but...'

'Use it.'

She felt surprised, and then realised it was rather a pleasant feeling of surprise. Surely Brett Carpenter wasn't worried about her safety and wellbeing? She scanned his face. It was suddenly closed to her.

'If I only could get that pool fixed,' she said wistfully. 'If the guests had a pool to lounge around they'd probably be less inclined to hang around the corrals in their spare time. Also, I can plan quite a few pool activities, but if that doesn't work out I'll have to plan a few more things on your territory. Bull-dogging. Bronco-breaking. Calf-branding. Things like that.'

'That's blackmail,' he said darkly.

'Exactly.' She grinned at him.

'I'll try and have a look at the pool tomorrow,' he conceded wearily.

'Thank you so much. Now, what about my proposal?'

'I said September.'

'Fine, that gives me lots of time to buy a dress. Now what about my other proposal?'

'You're pretty quick, aren't you?'

'You just told me the only way to make a cowboy shut up is to beat him at his own game.'

'OK.' He picked up the sheaf of paper off the table, and knocked them back into shape. 'Some of this is pretty good. Some of it isn't. For example, a mini-rodeo is absolutely out of the question.'

'But that was my best idea!'

'It's not realistic. You can't have a bunch of green-horns holding a rodeo. You'd end up with a few corpses at the end.'

'But couldn't we teach our guests a few basic things and then have a rodeo? Not a big one necessarily, but——'

'Would you teach someone a few basic cuts, and then let them practice neuro-surgery? It takes years to become a serious competitor in a rodeo.'

'It doesn't have to be serious.'

'I said no.' His tone was suddenly curt.

'I guess I'd better cancel my order for big silver belt buckles,' she said, more hurt than she was going to let him see.

'Unless you want to give them out for eyelash flicking and sweet talking,' he agreed.

'Brett, that's it!'

'I beg your pardon?'

'Your problem is that you're far too serious, and don't have any imagination at all to speak of.'

'My problem? Funny, until you arrived I was bliss-fully unaware of having any problems.' His eyes slid to her lips again, then swiftly flicked away when she gave them a nervous lick.

'We don't have to have a *real* rodeo if it's just not practical. We could have a kind of fun rodeo. Catching greased pigs——'

'You're not bringing any pigs on to my ranch.'

'It's not your ranch.'

'Pigs over my dead body.'

'Brett, would you listen to what I'm saying? It's not the pigs, precisely, that I'm talking about.'

'I'm relieved to hear that.'

'It's having a bunch of fun things to do that kind of resemble a rodeo. Like we could dress somebody up as a cow and have a roping contest. Or use a calf. We could put a barrel in some water, with a saddle on it, and have people try and ride that. We could have a cow-pie throwing contest.'

'I think I'll try to be satisfied with the belt buckle I've got, but by all means you and the dudes go ahead.'

She rolled her eyes at him. 'The guests could practise all week for it, if we had enough events.'

'I guess you could use some gymkhana events,' he suggested reluctantly.

'Gymwhat?'

He explained to her some of the horseback games involved in a gymkhana. 'Blair could help them develop some of the basic horsemanship skills they'd need to play the games.'

'Perfect!' she said excitedly. 'Now you're getting the hang of it.'

'Yippie.'

'You'll have to work on that "yippie" quite a lot,' she reprimanded him lightly, riding the wave of her excitement. 'What about the overnight camp-out, using the horses? We could sleep under the stars——'

'It does rain here, occasionally,' he interjected drily.

She ignored him. 'And we could eat beans out of cans.'

'People would pay you for that?'

'And have a campfire and sing songs.'

'So what would you need from me?'

'Horses, and an extra cowboy, besides Blair. And you could come along and help us sing.'

'I've arranged the horses, and I can lend you one of the other guys once a week. I'll pass on "Sing-along-with-Mandy-Marlowe".'

'Two out of three ain't bad.' But again, she felt that whisper of hurt. Was it just her ideas he thought were beneath his contempt or was it her in general?

'Will you play baseball? I thought we could hold the game about mid-week. Maybe around Wednesday, every week, with a big wiener roast after.'

'I already told you I wasn't playing baseball.'

'Oh, right. It would cut in on your sour-ball-munching time.'

'Not to mention vinegar-drinking,' he added, unperturbed.

'You might have fun.'

'I have a bum knee.'

'You could be the umpire.'

'I said no.'

She was starting to recognise that that tone meant the discussion was finished.

She didn't need to be treated like an annoying gnat by anybody, and least of all not by this two-bit, lone-star cowboy with a tacky five-pound silver buckle on his belt!

'Why won't you at least give this a fighting chance?'

She watched the temper flare in his own eyes—cool green waters suddenly turning stormy and unpredictable. 'Ms Marlowe, you got your extra man. You got horses. I'm going to do what I can for the pool. Why do you want my soul?'

'I personally feel that anything worth doing is worth putting your whole heart and soul into.' She said this with a sniff and a toss of her head.

'Fine. The key word there is "worth". What is worth something to you is not necessarily worth anything to me.'

'What have you got against people having fun? You act like a . . . a sober-sided old mule!'

She could tell he was momentarily stunned. He was obviously not a man used to being addressed in quite those terms or that tone—which was probably why he felt entitled to act so superior to everyone else! He recovered quickly.

'Look, this sober-sided old mule has been running this ranch since I was twenty-one years old. That has worth to me. I've seen quite a few hare-brained schemes come and go, and you'll have to forgive me if I don't get too excited about them.

'I have nothing against people having fun, as long as that's not their entire life's pursuit. Sure, fun has a place. A small place in the jigsaw of life, but a place. Still, you'll pardon me if I don't stand up and cheer when I see good money being poured down the drain on ideas that haven't been properly thought out.'

'This idea has been thought out.' She said the words, but then suddenly she wasn't so sure. She didn't know for certain how much thought James had put into this project, but she did know for certain he was nearly as impulsive as she herself was.

'Yeah? Where's the research, then? Where has it been written down in black and white what all this is going to cost? Where's the feasibility study, and the marketing report, and the accountant's projections?'

'I don't know,' Mandy whispered.

'Look, rainbow socks aside——'

Self-consciously she tried to tug her jeans down over the neon rainbows at her ankles.

'—I occasionally think I see signs of intelligence under that mop of carrot-coloured curls.'

'How dare you, you horrible old grouch!' She said it because she had to say something. She couldn't just take that sitting down. But he was incredible in his controlled anger—as threatening and as thrilling as a summer electrical storm.

'Shut up and listen for a change, little Red. You tell me how a guest ranch is going to work out here. You've just found out you can't get the pool maintenance man in. Or staff to stay. The nearest airport is an hour and a half away. The last twenty miles of road into this place is like a little patch of hell. There isn't a tourist attraction much closer than Hawaii. If one of your greenhorns gets hurt—and people who don't know what they're doing do get hurt on ranches—the nearest medical aid is a long way away.'

'Oh,' she said weakly.

'And if that isn't enough, the wind blows all the time. How do you like the wind so far?'

She didn't reply.

'And you ain't seen nothing yet. You should see what that wind can do to a nice little wienie roast, or to an overnight camping trip. Your little dudes will find their sleeping bags in Montana.

'So, pardon me if I'm not doing cartwheels because an ill-thought-out idea that I frankly feel is entirely unfeasible is being imposed on me against my will for the summer.'

What he didn't admit, and wasn't going to now, was that, reading her proposal, he'd been coaxed into a reluctant admiration of her. She did have good ideas. They had to be tempered with reality, of course, but she knew how to use her imagination to create something where nothing had been before.

By the time he'd finished reading her material he'd found himself agreeing to baseball games, barbecues, a community dance once in the summer, trail-rides, over-night camp-outs, and a host of other things. Now she had him agreeing to this play rodeo as well.

He'd given all the ground he was going to. He handed her back her papers. 'Look, I've marked on there what you can and can't do. I don't have any more time to talk about it today.'

'Here's the guest list as it stands for the summer,' she said, the chill in her tone not masking her hurt one little bit. 'I hope those weeks near the end fill out a bit more, but I think these bookings are pretty good, given that the idea is just getting off the ground.'

He glanced at the guest list. 'It looks not bad on paper,' he said. 'But so did Safari Land.'

'What?'

'Nothing.' The names on the list were largely European. Maybe that was why her name danced out at him, filled his whole vision.

Lillian Merriweather.

He stared at the name for a long time. A long time ago, before she'd married that doctor in Calgary, it had been a different name. Lillian Prentiss.

Why was she coming back here? After all these years?

'Is something wrong?'

He'd just been a beast to her so he didn't like the way the genuine concern in her voice made him feel. 'My leg just had one of those funny little twitches in it,' he lied.

He glanced up at those penetrating green eyes. He suddenly felt cranky. 'Are we done?' he snapped. God, he'd given a lot of ground. Green-eyed little witch had probably put some sort of spell on him.

The way Lillian used to do? a little voice inside his head mocked him.

With any luck this whole idea would have folded before the last week in July when Lillian was supposed to arrive. Mandy could have all the good ideas she wanted, but if the resort end of the ranch was going to be managed poorly it wouldn't float.

Given the young Lord Snow-Pollington's track record it would be more surprising if one of his schemes did work.

Meanwhile, the little leprechaun across from him looked like she was going to cry. Well, tough. Didn't she say she had some hairy boyfriend tucked away somewhere? Let her take her disappointments to him.

Now she was tilting that pert little nose up at the ceiling, and doing her best to look brave.

'The wedding,' she announced with theatrical censure, 'is off.'

'Maybe it's just as well. I don't want to have to deal with a jealous bear of a jilted boyfriend named Henry.'

'Harold,' she corrected him.

'Hmm. What does Harold think of James?'

He watched with interest as a delicate pink blush crept up the white of her skin. She was an attractive woman. It wasn't any of his concern if she had two or three, or a dozen men on a string at a time. As long as he wasn't one of them.

Still, he didn't like the idea of a beautiful woman being alone in that big old house with a creep like Felix gliding around.

'Actually, you might say James introduced me to Harold.'

On the other hand, she could probably handle herself quite nicely. It sounded as if she juggled the complexities of men with ease. Why did he find that so bloody annoying?

Brett had sweat dripping down his face and grease falling in his eyes. He was lying on his back and he dropped the wrench with a grunt, and peered again at the diagram of the pump. He said a few choice swear words.

There was nothing he hated worse than mechanics, unless it was...

'Brett? Are you in there?'

...A certain manipulative green-eyed monster. His first instinct was not to answer. Maybe if he just lay here quietly she would go away and leave the horrible, vinegar-drinking, sour-ball-munching old grouch alone.

The door to the pump house swung open and a shaft of daylight pierced the gloom.

'Oh, there you are.'

'Sober-sided mule that I am.'

'What?'

'Nothing.'

A nice scent wafted in, over the musty smell of the room. The smell of soap and sunshine, the delicate, good smells of a woman.

'I brought you a soda and some sandwiches.'

He sat up so fast he hit his head on a pipe. He cursed roundly.

'What the hell did you do that for?'

'I—I thought you might be hungry. You've been in here all morning.'

'Are you spying again?' He shot her a quick look. The sun was at her back, streaming through a too-large shirt, and outlining the full, lush curves of her figure. He scowled at the pump.

'No! I just noticed you come in here this morning.'

He didn't want her being nice to him. It made him feel like a project. As if she was single-handedly going to coax the nice guy out of the offensive grouch.

'Thanks,' he said grouchily, 'Just leave them there.'

'But they're warm. Herman just made them.'

'Herman?' He gave her an astounded look. 'Did you find a new chef already?'

She grinned. Her teeth were straight and white. He had a sudden memory of how her teeth had felt that day he kissed her.

'You call him Croc. That's a terrible thing to call a nice man.'

'And a nice thing to call a terrible man.' He felt utterly betrayed. And more suspicious than ever. It was obviously part of her life's mission to turn crotchety old loners into congenial citizens whom she could make eat out of the palm of her hand.

Small hands, pink on one side and freckled on the other. He remembered what they'd felt like as they tightened on his shoulders. He wondered what they'd feel like wrapped wantonly around his neck.

'I'm losing my marbles,' he muttered, giving the pump a vicious smash with the wrench. It hummed to life.

'Is it working?'

He stared at the thing, astounded. 'It appears to be.'

'Good. You can come eat your lunch, and I'll keep you company.'

'I don't like company.'

'Oh, pooh. You've been out on the range too long. I'm certainly more interesting than a cow.' She wrinkled her nose at him. 'And better-looking, too.'

She was absolutely right, he thought. He'd been alone too long. That was why this green-eyed menace was looking so appealing today, making him think renegade thoughts.

He followed her out of the pool house. She plopped herself down on a piece of dry-looking grass, and hugged her knees. The sunlight tangled in her red curls. She was wearing blue denim shorts that revealed far too much of her slender, freckled legs. She was also wearing socks with little red pom-poms hanging off them.

He looked longingly down the road towards the relative safety of his house. What he needed right now was a long, cold shower, or a long, hard ride. He glanced just as longingly at the sandwiches she had brought. Breakfast seemed as if it had been a miserably long time ago. The battle was brief. He sank down beside her. He picked up a sandwich and bit into it.

Croc had risen to new heights. The sandwich was ambrosia. Green-eyed little witch.

She was quiet, for once.

'How old are you, Brett?'

He should have known it was too good to last. 'A hundred and six.'

'No, *really*,' she chided.

He looked at her. Old enough to know that after what had happened in his bedroom that day they couldn't go backwards.

They couldn't sit here on the lawn and pretend it hadn't happened.

'Old enough to know better,' he said, putting the sandwich down.

CHAPTER FOUR

'DON'T go. It was just a question.'

But he was already standing up. He was dressed differently today. A faded baseball cap that proclaimed him a Blue Jays fan covered his black hair. Instead of a Western shirt he was wearing a grey sweatshirt with ragged edges at the shoulders where the sleeves had been torn off.

Those protruding arms were disconcertingly masculine: tanned, muscular, sprinkled with fine dark hairs.

'I have some other things to do.'

'Twenty-nine.'

'How did you know that?' he asked with dry surprise.

He had a spot of grease to one side of his nose. She resisted a funny urge to stand up and wipe the smudge off.

'I have a system for guessing,' she said lightly. 'I multiply the number of grey hairs by ten then divide by two and then add nine.'

'How many grey hairs does that leave me with?' he asked. A reluctant smile was tugging at the firm edges of his mouth.

'Four,' she teased him.

'I'm sure there will be more before the summer is over.' He regarded her solemnly. 'You must know quite a few men if you've come up with such an effective method for guessing age.'

He was still looking restless and edgy, as though he were going to bolt for the barn at any minute. Didn't he understand that they had to form a co-operative relationship if they were going to keep both their grey-hair counts to a minimum this summer?

'It is very old-fashioned to assume a woman who has many friendships with men is loose, fast, or criminal.' She sighed. Despite her best intentions she could hear an edge in her voice. Why did he make her so angry?

'Is that right?' he said. His eyes had narrowed to slits. 'How many friendships do you have with men?'

'Well, there's my principal at school——'

'At school?' he gasped. 'Murphy S. Jones! How *old* are you?'

'Oh, for heaven's sake,' she said with disgust. 'I *teach* at school. I'm not a student. I'm twenty-seven.'

He stared at her. '*You're* twenty-seven? *You're* a teacher?'

'Kindergarten.'

'You don't look a day over twenty-one.'

'I know. I was raised on sunscreen and broad-brimmed hats. One of the hazards of being a red-head.'

'Twenty-seven *and* a teacher?' he asked again, incredulously.

'Is it so surprising to you that I'm a respectable member of society?' she asked, not all of her indignation faked.

'Yes.'

'Well, that was blunt.' She might have been more offended than she was, except for the unfathomable light that was darkening his eyes, that clear jade becoming smoky. Had it just occurred to him that she was mature? Not a pesky irritant, but a mature, sensual woman?

His gaze was hooded now, whatever light she had seen there had been promptly squelched.

'I'm glad you have something to fall back on,' he said gruffly, 'when this doesn't pan out.'

She jerked her chin upwards. 'I keep telling you I'm going to *make* this pan out.'

He eyed her with an amusement she found extremely annoying. 'How can you make it to twenty-seven and still be filled with fire-and-brimstone enthusiasm for hare-brained plots?'

'Some people don't stop believing in dreams. I despise cynicism.'

An unconcerned smile played briefly across the altogether too sexy contours of his mouth. 'This land does that to people. "Cynical" isn't the word I'd use. Realistic, maybe.'

'And hard?' she suggested.

He nodded without offence. 'Yeah. And hard. Thanks for bringing me lunch. The pool just has to be vacuumed and it'll be ready for your guests.'

'Thank you.' She rose too, for a reason she did not understand not wanting him to go. Possibly because he was the only human in about a hundred square miles that she found interesting to talk to. Challenging. Marlowes did have that weakness for a challenge.

He gazed at her for a moment, and then suddenly his brow furrowed and he frowned.

'How did you really know I was twenty-nine?'

She felt uncomfortable under his penetrating eye.

'You've been snooping through the files in the office, haven't you?'

'Not your office!'

'The one in the big house?'

'James told me to use whatever I needed,' Mandy said defensively.

'And you *needed* a graze through the filing cabinet?'

'I was checking to see if Felix had any credentials, actually, and I encountered your name on my way to his. I just had a little look.' His age. His marital status. His yearly evaluations. His family history was pretty much entwined with the ranch. A little look. What was an hour in the course of a life, after all?

Brett was looking at her with naked dislike.

She sighed. Any ground she had gained with the sandwiches had just been lost. A less stalwart type might be willing to concede the whole war to Brett if they went by the intimidating chilliness that had entered his eyes.

'And what did you find out about Felix?' he asked grimly.

She suspected he was not letting her off the hook, but grabbed eagerly at the change of subject. 'He doesn't seem very well qualified for his job.'

'Do you smell the coffee yet?' he asked sharply.

'I don't know what you mean.'

'In my world,' he said tersely, 'when we want to know something more about a person, we generally just out and ask, as rustic as that must seem to people like you and the young lord.'

She could understand him branding her, but why James?

'I shouldn't have looked at your personal file,' she said contritely. 'I'm sorry.'

'You know, lady, an apology goes a long way when a person admits they are wrong, and with that admission comes a sincere attempt to change the behaviour. But don't waste your breath apologising when tomorrow you'll probably be phoning my mother to dig out a few more kernels of information about me.'

'You are not that fabulously interesting!' she informed him, stung, but she remembered, with a touch of shame, that she had looked at his mother's name and phone number, listed under who to contact in case of an emergency, with some interest.

'Good. I'm glad to hear you don't think so. Perhaps I can look forward to a tiny bit of privacy over this horrible summer.'

'It won't be horrible, you miserable old goat, and a little curiosity is a sign of an active mind.'

'And a lot kills the cat,' he said with a fair degree of menace. 'With eyes the colour of yours, you could take that as a warning.'

'One would almost think you were guarding some deep, dark secret,' she told him haughtily.

'I am,' he said, and suddenly he was standing very close to her.

She could feel his bristling physical presence. He smelled good—like sunshine and soap and sweat all mingled together in precisely the right proportions.

A strong hand went under her chin and without warning his mouth laid claim to hers.

She was shocked by the pure sensation of it. The first time he had kissed her it had been tantalisingly gentle. This kiss was ruthless and demanding. It took, and gave nothing back. He forced her lips open and plunged the molten hot spear of his tongue into the hollow of her mouth.

Liquid heat curled upwards from her toes to her knees to that sensitive, secret spot at her core. The fire ignited in her belly and her breasts. She sagged against him in a surrender of passion.

He shoved her limp form, none too gently, away from him.

She looked at him with dazed, drugged eyes.

'That's the secret,' he said coldly.

'What?' she whispered dazedly. The coldness in his eyes was in such contrast to the heat he had created that she felt unnerved, completely lost in time and space.

'A man like me eats little girls like you for lunch,' he informed her coldly. 'Don't forget it. And don't push over my boundaries again.'

She could feel the sharp ache of tears behind her eyes. She blinked furiously.

'I'm twenty-seven,' she reminded him, fighting for a note of amused disdain. 'I've been kissed once or twice before. You won't be having me for lunch, because I'm not on the stupid menu.'

Intensity turned his eyes from green to greener, and she thought she had probably failed to fool him. He turned abruptly and walked away, his stride smooth and relaxed, supremely, maddeningly confident.

'You kiss like a three-hundred-year-old platypus,' she called after him. 'I think it's very unlikely you'll find your boundaries stormed in the middle of the night— unless it's by one of your cows!'

He didn't even glance back at her, and she eyed the crockery from lunch with severe temptation to aim it squarely at the back of his head.

But then he might guess that he didn't kiss like a three-hundred-year-old platypus after all!

*   *   *

Mandy watched from the porch as the first bus load full of guests pulled up in front of the house.

The bus, she decided with a sigh, was a disaster. But then so was Felix. And the majority of the guest-rooms. What on earth had James been thinking of when he had given her the best room in the house instead of reserving it, and rightfully so, for a paying guest?

She sighed and finished enumerating the disasters. The wind. The unrelenting emptiness of the countryside. The plumbing. And her relationship with Brett. Her non-relationship with Brett. Disastrous.

For the first time, she was facing a first day with guests with a heavy feeling in her heart, and a funny unfamiliar anxiety knotting her stomach.

She pasted on a smile, and swung down the steps to the bus. The door creaked open. 'Welcome to the Big——'

Sploosh!

A pudgy adolescent boy with a machine-gun shaped water pistol that seemed to have held at least a gallon of water grinned evilly at her.

She stood there, her smile frozen, her hair ruined, water dripping down her face, her blouse plastered to her.

'This place looks like a pit,' the boy announced in a very British accent. He jumped down off the bus steps and roared by her, heading straight for the corrals.

'Stop!' she yelled desperately. He heard, but didn't listen. She sighed. Unless she missed her guess, she was about to get another black mark beside her name in Brett's book.

'Well,' she muttered, 'in that case, give him a squirt for me, too.'

Sighing again, pasting her smile back on, she turned to greet her next guest.

Her smile wobbled, and then broke. 'Charity,' she whispered. A ray of delight partially dissipated that bleak cloud that had been hanging around the vicinity of her heart. She looked into her cousin's familiar, gentle features and felt as if she could cry from happiness.

In Charity's arms was a squirming blue bundle from which faint noises were emerging.

Charity came down the steps and Mandy hugged her, and peeped at the baby's cranky little features.

'Goodness, he looks just the way Matthew looked the day he caught you spying on him, Charity.'

Charity laughed, but the weariness was evident in her features. 'Greet your other guests, and then we'll talk.'

'Thanks,' Mandy said. Somehow her energy had returned. She greeted the guests with genuine warmth, and then handed them over to Felix, who she was sure had managed to thoroughly botch all the room assignments.

Still, it gave her time to sit across from Charity in the big roomy dining-room. They put the baby on the table between them where they could both admire him while they chatted.

'What are you doing here?' Mandy asked, thrilled.

'I ran into James in London, and when he found out I was going to be in Canada at Anpetuwi for most of the summer, he insisted I accept a few weeks' stay here as a gift.'

Mandy felt a stab of discomfort. 'He gave you a vacation at the ranch?'

'Unbelievably generous, wasn't it?'

'Unbelievably,' Mandy murmured uneasily. Unbelievably un-businesslike.

'I think it's a measure of his caring for you, Mandy.
He might have suspected you were lonely here. Goodness,
it's lonely country, isn't it? Still, I just couldn't pass up
the opportunity to see you. I might have though, had I
known what that bus trip was going to be like! Honestly,
I think crossing the Sahara by camel would have been
more comfortable.'

Mandy felt another stab of discomfort. Wasn't that
one of the concerns Brett had named when he was
making his case for why the Big Bar L *wouldn't* make
a good guest ranch?

Firmly, Mandy pushed her discomfort to the back of
her mind. Charity was here, now. Mandy had never felt
like she needed a friend more.

'And Matthew thought it might be good for Tim.'

'Tim?' Mandy knew the baby's name was Matthew,
Junior.

'Tim.' Charity looked troubled. 'The young hellion
who blasted you with his water gun. I'm sorry about
that.'

'It's not for you to be sorry. Who is he?'

'He's Matthew's nephew. His father was a fighter
pilot. He was killed. Tim hasn't handled it well.
Everybody keeps thinking he'll get better, but he doesn't.
He gets worse and worse. His poor mother needed a
break from him, so we offered to take him to Anpetuwi
for the summer. He's nearly dismantled it, so we thought
maybe the wide open spaces...'

'Poor kid,' Mandy said with real feeling, forgiving
him for the blouse that was still clinging to
her uncomfortably.

'I know. It's sad, isn't it?' Charity fixed her lovely blue eyes on Mandy. 'Speaking of poor kids, are you all right? I've never seen you look so...subdued.'

On anybody else, Mandy might have tried to pooh-pooh that observation, but there was no sense even trying with Charity. Her cousin saw everything.

'There's a man here who kind of gets under my skin,' she admitted softly.

'A man who gets under *your* skin?' Charity echoed, her eyes widening. 'That must be some man.'

'Oh, he's a brute. He's bad-tempered and ill-humoured, totally unreasonable——'

'Good-looking, I'll assume,' Charity interrupted solemnly.

'Some might think so,' Mandy said with an airy lack of interest, 'if you like the type. You know, big, and muscular and tanned, green eyes, jet-black hair.'

'Oh,' Charity said softly. 'That type. The type that any female who breathes likes.'

Mandy glared at her, and then burst out laughing. 'Is that any way for a happily married woman to talk?'

'I was speaking from a strictly professional point of view.'

'Of course you were.'

'Auntie Char-I-TEE!' The call was a combination between a banshee wail and a shriek.

Charity shook her head. 'He must have found trouble. He only calls me that when he's in trouble. Generally I'm Dr Dweeb to him.'

The boy, Tim, burst through the doors. 'There's an awful man chasing me. I think he intends to kill me. Save me, Aunt Char.'

The door burst open again, and Brett Carpenter stood there, magnificent in his anger.

So magnificent that Tim apparently gave up any hope of his aunt being able to save him, and pounded out of the door through the kitchen.

Mandy could only hope Brett would follow him.

'You have had guests here for exactly ten minutes,' Brett said descending on Mandy, fury in every line of that well-honed face. 'And we've already had an accident. I told you to keep people the hell away from the corrals.'

She prayed he'd take up the chase again, but instead he yanked out the chair beside her and collapsed into it. He swore softly and colourfully under his breath.

'I don't care how mad you are,' Mandy said, deciding the offensive might be a better tactic than sitting here waiting for his wrath to descend. 'That kind of language is——'

'He's hurt,' Charity interrupted. 'Let me look at that.'

For the first time, Mandy noticed the dark red stain spreading across the front of Brett's shirt. A quick gasp of horror escaped her. Her eyes flew to his face. She noticed, suddenly how pale he was, his eyes now shut.

'Do you suppose he's dying?' she whispered.

'Am I allowed to swear if I am?' he asked cynically, opening one eye and regarding her.

'I guess you're not dying.'

'Better luck next guest,' he retorted.

'Do you think I could have a look at your injury?' Charity interrupted impatiently.

Brett eyed Charity warily, apparently not nearly as comfortable being rude to her as he was being rude to Mandy.

'He's very sensitive about having strange woman see his chest,' Mandy explained. 'Brett, this is my cousin, Charity Blake. She's a doctor. Charity, Brett Carpenter. He's the ranch foreman . . . and head grouch.'

Brett regarded Charity with interest. 'Beauty runs in the family,' Brett said softly. Mandy was astonished by his easy country charm.

For a moment, Mandy almost liked him. Not because of the back-handed compliment to her, but because few men recognised Charity's understated beauty. Who would have expected Brett Carpenter to have a gift for spotting that elusive concept of quality that Charity had?

He unbuttoned his shirt, wincing as he pulled it away from the already clotting blood.

'Ooooh,' Mandy breathed, when she saw the long, ragged cut beneath his right pectoral muscle.

'See, Mandy? The man has a perfect right to be a little grouchy.' To him, Charity said, 'I'll bet that hurts, doesn't it?'

'A mere scratch, ma'am,' he said sardonically. He clenched his teeth as Charity gently probed the wound. 'Mandy, would you fetch my black bag? It's still in the bus.'

'Before you faint,' he suggested, looking at her with disgust.

'Hah! As if I'd waste a good faint on a mere scratch.'

Still, she went gladly for the bag, far more upset by Brett's wound than she wanted him to see. For one panicked moment, seeing that large, powerful form so vulnerable, seeing the pain so clearly in those strong features, she really had thought he must be dying. Silly to blurt it out like that. The arrogant ass might think she cared.

Did she care? The air outside cleared her head. Of course she didn't want *anyone* dying the first day of operations. That's what had caused that aching fear to leap so suddenly in her breast, that panic to claw momentarily at her throat.

When she returned Charity had Brett completely at ease. They were chatting like old friends.

Mandy's eyes drifted back to his chest. It was the first close-up look she'd had of it. The perfect cut of the chest suggested it might have been carved from marble, an illusion tempered somewhat by the blood dripping down it.

'What happened, anyway?'

She couldn't take her eyes off his chest, though she had to admit to herself that phenomena probably had less to do with the wound than the awesome perfection of that part of his anatomy.

'I was halter-training a filly. The idiot boy shot her with a water gun. She leaped sideways and rammed me into a fence that a nail had worked out of.'

'Oh, Brett, I'm sorry.'

He glared at her. 'That helps a whole hell of a lot.'

She coloured uncomfortably, remembering what he thought her apologies were worth.

'It's my fault entirely,' Charity said quietly. 'Tim is my nephew and my responsibility.' She had swabbed off his chest, and now was applying butterfly sutures to the cut.

Brett's admiration for her showed in his eyes. 'You know, you could teach your cousin a thing or two.'

'What does that mean?' Mandy demanded crossly.

'It means that accepting responsibility is a sign of maturity and strength. You're responsible for your guests.

And not because of my safety, though I wouldn't mind that being a consideration, but for their own.'

'I could hardly have prevented that child from leaping off the bus,' Mandy said tersely. 'He stampeded right over me.'

'You could go with the bus to pick up the guests, you know. That would give you a long time to set down ground rules, before people even got here.'

She stared at him, hating to admit what a good idea that was.

To add insult to her injury, Charity betrayed her by laughing. 'Mr Carpenter——'

'Brett,' he corrected easily.

'Far better people than me have tried to tame Mandy...'

Mandy gave Charity a hard kick under the table. Charity didn't even flinch.

'...without, I'm pleased to say, too much success. I know she's irrepressible and impulsive. She's altogether too curious, and many times she acts before she thinks. She likes to be the centre of attention. She's too certain of her right to have things her own way.'

'Right on,' Brett breathed with satisfaction.

'Charity!' Mandy protested, humiliated.

'However,' Charity continued with a broad wink at Brett, 'in the final analysis, Mandy has what I consider to be the most important of our human qualities. She is capable of great kindness. She also has a *joie de vivre* like few people I have ever met, and we more sober-sided folk can generally learn quite a lot from her attitude towards life... if we let ourselves.'

Brett looked at Charity thoughtfully, and then his gaze drifted to Mandy.

'Little leprechaun,' he said, with a rueful shake of his dark curls.

'That's a slight improvement over "green-eyed monster",' Mandy said with a toss of her head.

'Careful, Brett,' Charity cautioned him lightly. 'She'll put a spell on you.'

'Not likely,' he said. 'I seem to be the only person around here immune to her charms, considerable as they might be.'

'Quit talking about me as if I weren't here!' Mandy protested, her face hot with embarrassment.

'There,' Charity said, looking at Brett's chest with satisfaction. 'All done.'

He stood up and buttoned up his shirt. 'Thank you.' He winced. 'I don't suppose I'm going to catch that boy today.'

'What were you going to do with him if you caught him anyway?' Mandy asked suspiciously.

Brett grinned. 'Suffice to say it's rather fortunate I didn't catch him in the heat of my rage.'

'Neanderthal,' Mandy sputtered.

'And I'm not sure how safe he'll be when I do catch up with him.'

'Don't you dare do anything to Tim!'

Brett's mouth tightened into a hard line. 'Fine. You do your job and I won't have to. I do expect the boy to be disciplined. What he did was dangerous. It can't be allowed to happen again.'

'Dealing with children happens to be one of my specialities,' Mandy told him tersely.

'Dealing with an out-of-control adolescent is slightly different than dealing with a wayward five-year-old.'

'Thank you for sharing that with me. Would you like to suggest a suitable punishment, as well? Tickle torture, perhaps? Hanging him by his thumbs until he pleads for mercy?'

Brett glared at her, the light in his eyes nothing short of dangerous. 'I deal with men. That's my job. I know how to do it.'

'Tim is more boy than man. I think the gentle approach would be better than whatever you have in mind.'

'Your arrogance is unbelievable.'

Charity interceded, the epitome of calm. 'Really, you two, please don't use Tim as an excuse to argue with each other, as satisfying as that appears to be for both of you. He's my responsibility and I'll look after it.'

Brett looked at Charity, a faintly sheepish grin toyed at the edges of his mouth. 'Do you prefer Mrs Blake, or Dr Blake?'

'Charity,' she insisted.

Mandy felt this funny little worm of envy at the easy rapport that had developed so quickly between Brett and Charity.

'I trust you, Charity, to let your nephew know the seriousness of what happened today.'

Mandy gave him a dirty look. He was treating Charity like a respected member of a team—an attitude she, Mandy, deserved, since she was the one who had to work with the boor.

'Thank you. If I need any help dealing with him, I'll let you know.'

'Him?' Mandy squeaked.

'Mandy, I think maybe he's right. I don't think the gentle approach is working on Tim. He might need a man's hand right now.'

Brett gave Mandy a look that was arrogantly smug. 'I'll be glad to help in any way I can.'

Mandy wanted to strangle him. How dared he con her cousin into thinking he was a nice guy?

'Thank you, though I hope I won't have to ask, and I hope Tim won't bother you again.'

'I hope not. As for you,' Brett said, giving Mandy a look that said clearly he thought her cousin was a *real* woman, 'I want every guest assembled in this room within the next few minutes. You make it clear to them where they are allowed to go and where they aren't, what they're allowed to do, and what they aren't. Do I make myself clear?'

His high-handed tone made her feel furious, but she knew his request was not an unreasonable one.

'Yes, sir,' she said with an angry toss of her head.

'Charity, thank you for the doctoring. I hope you're staying for a long time, because I have a feeling this won't be the last accident.' He sent Mandy another meaningful look.

She wanted to cross her eyes and stick out her tongue at him, but she didn't want one single thing that Charity had said about her to prove true.

When Brett left, she glared at her cousin. 'You betrayed me.'

'Don't be silly,' Charity said placidly.

'Those were awful things you said about me!'

'We all have faults, Mandy. Most of us just keep them hidden a little better than you do. I didn't say one thing to Brett that he hadn't already thought for himself.'

'That's true,' Mandy said glumly. 'He doesn't think much of me.'

'Then he's not as smart as he looks. I bet he thinks more of you than he's letting on.'

'That would be a losing bet.'

Charity smiled, a tiny, knowing smile that was extremely irritating. 'Do you remember how Matthew and I squabbled last summer, Mandy?'

Mandy allowed a smile to be coaxed out of her. 'Yes. Honestly, it was so funny seeing you, normally so self-contained, all tied up in knots like that all the time.' She saw suddenly what Charity was getting at. 'Oh, this is nothing like that.'

'It isn't?'

'No! I mean the sexual sizzle when you and Matthew were in the same room was so obvious to everybody.'

'Except to me and Matthew.'

'Take it from me, Charity, Brett Carpenter hates my guts.'

'My, that's a strong reaction from a man who seems so reasonable.'

'He's not at all reasonable,' Mandy said crossly. 'He just put on a big act for you.'

'Why would he do that?'

'Oh, you know people are always trying to impress doctors.'

'I've never seen a man less likely to put himself out to impress others.'

'Humph. When did you become such an expert on men?'

Charity ignored her ill humour and gave her a probing look. 'And do you hate his guts, as well?'

'Oh, absolutely!'

'Hmm.'

'Charity, there's nothing there!'

'All right. I believe you.' Her tone said she believed no such thing. She paused and tucked a soft blanket more tightly around her sleeping baby.

'Besides, there's James,' Mandy said desperately.

'What about James?'

'He's crazy about me. Look, he even sent you to visit me.'

'That's quite different from visiting himself, isn't it?'

'I think James and I have the basis for a very meaningful relationship.'

Charity looked oddly unconvinced.

'Don't you like James?' Mandy pressed.

'I think he can be a lot of fun,' Charity said cautiously. 'He has many of the same qualities you have. He's very irrepressible and impulsive.'

'Sounds like a match made in heaven to me,' Mandy said lightly.

Charity didn't say anything.

'Surely you don't think Brett and I would be a good match!' she exclaimed horrified. 'We're the exact opposites. He wouldn't know how to have fun if it stepped on him. He's about as flexible as a rock. He's mulish, arrogant and rude. He's——'

'Unbelievably good-looking,' Charity interrupted with a smile.

'God took pity on him. A man with that many faults should have at least one redeeming quality. Anyway, it's wasted on him. What's the use of being so gloriously attractive in the middle of nowhere? And what's the use of having such a nice face if you're always going to spoil it with sour looks?'

'Tell me,' Charity said, ever so casually, 'has he ever kissed you?'

Mandy suddenly found herself cornered by laughing blue eyes. She opened her mouth to speak, but no sound came out.

Charity nodded sagely. 'Why don't you show me to my room now, and then I'll go see what I can do with my nephew?'

CHAPTER FIVE

Two days, Brett thought wearily. The main invasion had only been here for two days.

And it felt as if the Big Bar L was never going to be the same.

Brett glared at Bud's ankle. It was swollen to twice its normal size, and sported shades of green, purple and black.

'How did you do this?' he asked again. Bud had already told him, but there was the off-chance he had heard incorrectly.

'Playing baseball, boss. I tried to slide home.'

'Baseball,' he muttered. 'For God's sake, man, you do the roughest, toughest work on the face of the earth, and you do this to your ankle playing ball with children, blue-haired ladies and pot-bellied men? You've come out of busting broncs in better shape!'

'Mandy plays for keeps,' Bud said defensively.

Somehow Brett had known it was only a matter of time until *her* name came up. 'That explains it,' he said tightly. 'There's a doctor at the big house. Mandy's cousin, Charity. Maybe you could ask her to have a look at it for you. It just looks sprained to me, but maybe she should check for a break.'

'Mandy's cousin?' Bud said happily.

'Maybe I better go with him,' Mick volunteered.

'Get on your horse——' he put a few more expletives between 'your' and 'horse' than were strictly necessary '—and get to work,' he ordered Mick.

He turned back to Bud. 'Mandy's cousin is married. She's a lady. Use your manners.'

Use your manners. What was he running here, a Sunday school? He closed his eyes. Was life ever going to be the same? Pure? Sweet? Simple? So blessedly simple?

He'd looked up from his paper last night to see the faces of two kindly-looking old ladies pressed against his window. They were looking for the ball diamond.

He informed them it wasn't in his living-room. He could have left it at that, but he noticed they both looked tired and confused. The next thing he knew they were both sipping iced tea on his couch. Later he escorted them to the baseball diamond. So much for a quiet evening with the newspaper.

Yesterday, he'd been riding along trying to put some distance between himself and the chaos, that was very closely associated in his mind with that red-haired vixen, when he had seen a potato crisp bag stuck in a scraggly stand of aspens. A stand of aspens suspiciously close to where the morning trail ride had gone by. The fury he had felt had been cold and killing.

He gave the cinch on his saddle one final tug, and his horse snorted in surprise.

'Sorry,' he muttered. He put his boot in the stirrup and vaulted into the saddle. He turned the horse, expecting to see his men mounted as well.

Instead they were gathered in a silent circle.

He edged his horse into it. Mick was gingerly holding a bright red bikini top, and the other cowboys were standing around staring at it.

'Where did you get that?' Brett asked sternly.

'Just blowed up, boss. Just now. Nearly skeart Burt's horse into next week.'

'Do you suppose whoever lost it is at the pool?' Blair suggested. 'Do you suppose she maybe ain't even realised it's gone yet?'

It looked as if there was going to be a stampede towards the swimming pool.

'Get on your horses, *now*,' Brett ordered. He reached down, grabbed the slip of fabric from Mick and shoved it in the pocket of the windbreaker he'd worn today.

He whirled his horse and left the yard. Within seconds he could hear hoofbeats falling into place behind him.

And the men speaking in low undertones.

'Whose do ya suppose it is?'

'Mandy's?' was one seemingly hopeful suggestion.

That name again, Brett thought grimly.

'Nah, Mandy wouldn't wear red, would she? With her hair like that?'

'Too big for her anyway,' another voice commented. 'I bet it was that blonde girl that played second base last night. She was a comely——'

'The next man,' Brett said quietly, keeping his eyes front, 'who says one more word this morning about baseball, bikinis, blondes or Mandy Marlowe, is going to be up to his ass in cow crap until next Christmas, understood?'

There was surprised silence from behind him. And then one quiet mutter of protest.

'Gee, what's gotten into him?'

Brett nudged his horse into a gallop. What *had* gotten into him? He didn't talk to his men like that. He suspected it had something to do with that little slip of red fabric in his pocket. Ever since somebody had suggested it might be hers, it felt as if it was burning him right through his jacket.

The same way her lips had burned against his. The same way her eyes burned at the back of his mind. The same way *he* burned when he remembered the soft swell of her breasts crushed into his chest.

Damn, but it was going to be a one long hot summer on this ranch. One sizzling summer.

Later that day, he stood in the shadow of the porch, looking in the dining-room window of the big house. He'd been on his way to find Mandy when the music and movement had stopped him. He'd paused to take one glimpse and somehow not moved again.

The tables had all been cleared away, and music was blaring.

'One, two, three, kick,' Mandy called, 'then back, two, three, kick.'

She was teaching some kind of dance. Line dancing, he thought he had heard it called. She was wearing tight jeans, a brown Western shirt with lavish white fringes, a cowboy hat and cowboy boots. She should have looked ridiculous. She looked stunning.

'Then wiggle, wiggle, whoopee,' she said doing something so outrageous with her hips that Brett felt his mouth go dry.

Everybody was laughing, and clapping and having a wonderful time.

He felt the oddest squeeze deep in his belly. Not a physical squeeze. Not this time.

He'd lived here in this big, lonely country all his life, and never once felt lonely. What was that little pixie doing to him?

In the back of his mind, he registered a baby crying, but at first he didn't think anything of it. But then he noticed Charity in there dancing.

She had looked as if she had more sense, he thought, but then she also looked as if she was having fun. She looked like the type of woman who needed to have more fun.

And Mandy was just the one to coax her into doing it.

But where was the baby? Those howls sounded like they were coming from outside. He walked towards the sound, came around the corner of the house, and stopped dead in his tracks.

The baby was sitting in a high chair in the middle of the lawn, while the boy, *that* boy, aimed that squirt gun at him. He mostly missed, but when he hit the baby howled with chagrin.

Brett hadn't been able to catch him once, but he wasn't going to let him get away this time.

He came off the veranda like a bullet exploding out of a gun. The boy was so absorbed in his sport he didn't see him until it was too late.

'What the hell is the matter with you?' Brett demanded, grabbing the boy by his collar.

The boy looked at him with defiance, and then at the soaking wet, wailing baby. Shame tinged his features.

'I don't know,' he said softly. 'I just don't know.'

*   *   *

'Wiggle,' Mandy panted, throwing her hips right. 'Wiggle,' she said, throwing them left, 'and whoopee!' she said rotating them in a circle.

There was general uproar as the line dancers threw their hips the wrong way and collapsed in helpless giggles on the 'whoopee'.

'One more time,' she called, above the music and the laughter and the voices. 'We've almost got it.'

'We've almost got a hernia,' somebody yelled back at her.

'We'll rename it the Hernia Hoopla, just for you, Maxine,' Mandy called good-naturedly. 'OK, everybody together. Wiggle, wiggle——'

'Miss Marlowe.'

His voice cut easily through all the noise.

She whirled, and the laughter died in her throat. Brett Carpenter stood framed in the doorway, looking every inch a cowboy, except for the incongruous fact he had baby Matthew Blake tucked under one arm like a football, and Tim Blake held firmly by the other. Both Blake boys had tearstained faces.

She turned and flipped off the tape, then turned back.

'What have you done?' she asked, scanning Tim's face with horror. This was a boy who did not cry.

'What have I done?' he asked in a low voice, incredulous with fury.

Charity was right behind her, rescuing Matthew from under the big arm.

'What on earth is going on here?' Mandy demanded, planting her hands firmly on her hips.

'I think you and I need to talk…privately,' Brett said, nodding toward the very interested dancers watching them. 'You'd better come too, Charity.'

Mandy noted she was Miss Marlowe, but Charity wasn't Dr Blake.

She turned back to the guests. 'OK, cowboys and cowgirls, back to the Hip-Swinging Hoopla. I want it perfect when I get back. No root beer and doughnuts for anybody who fails to meet my exacting standards.'

She turned the music back on. But not loud enough to miss what Brett muttered under his breath.

'Your exacting standards,' he said, with such venom Mandy felt like she'd been hit.

'All right,' she said, closing the office door behind them. 'What is going on? What did you do to Timmy?'

'Which one's Timmy?' Brett asked. Fire was coming out his eyes, even though his tone was level.

'Him.' Mandy noticed the boy had started to shake with reaction. 'And I think you can let him go now.'

Brett ignored that suggestion. 'Tim, why don't you tell them what I did to you, then your Aunt Mandy can decide whether to have me or you cup up in small pieces and fed to the coyotes.'

'He hit me,' the boy wailed. 'He bashed me right in the chops as hard as he could. I was knocked out for a full minute!'

'You brute!' Mandy said to Brett in an outraged whisper. 'I'm not going to have you fed to the coyotes. I'm going to——'

'Where is the bruise?' Charity asked wearily.

'Huh?' Tim grunted.

'If a man built like Mr Carpenter hits you, you have something to show for it. Your "chops" look OK to me.'

'Son——'

'I'm not your son!' Tim screamed at Brett with such vehemence that for a moment a stunned silence fell over the room.

Something changed in Brett at that moment. Mandy wasn't sure what. The sternness did not leave his features, nor did his grip on Tim's arm loosen, but a hint of compassion took the hard glitter out of those green eyes.

'Tell us what really happened,' he said, and the firmness in his voice brooked no nonsense.

'I offered to look after Matthew for Doctor Dwe—I mean Aunt Char, kind of as penance like for squirting the horse with the gun and making it squash you.'

'That's very commendable,' Mandy said encouragingly.

Brett shot her a black look that said as clearly as if he had spoken *shut up*.

'Then, when everybody was dancing, I took him outside. I was going to play with him, but he's not a lot of fun, you know? So, I found his high chair and put him in it, and kind of, like, used him as a target for my water gun.'

Charity stared at her nephew. 'How could you do such a thing?'

Mandy wondered how Brett had managed to restrain himself from busting the boy a good one in the chops.

Tim started to shake again. 'I don't know why I did it. I don't know why I'm so bad.' He started to cry, and the three adults stood there staring at him, and at each other, helplessly.

Brett let go of his arm. 'Bring me the squirt gun,' he said quietly.

The boy looked at him with pleading, and then left to retrieve it off the lawn.

'Brett, I'm sorry. I practically accused you of abusing the boy,' Mandy said.

'You know, if you'd stop and think for just three seconds before you jumped right in, you wouldn't end up apologising nearly so much.'

Charity laughed, and Mandy glared at her.

'Brett, I have to apologise, too,' Charity said. 'I thought I'd dealt with him, but I can see I didn't do it very well.'

Tim returned. His head down, he handed over the squirt gun to Brett.

Neatly, Brett broke it over his knee.

'Mister!'

'Brett, don't you think that's a little harsh?' Mandy asked.

He gave her a quelling look. 'We don't give two warnings in ranch country,' he told the boy. 'Now go to your room. And don't leave it until your aunt tells you you can, and tells you how you're going to be punished.'

The boy looked sullenly at his destroyed gun. 'Isn't that punishment enough?'

'No,' Brett said.

'Brett,' Mandy said after Tim had left, 'don't be so hard on him. He's lost his father.'

'Well, then his mother has had enough grief,' Brett said unemotionally. 'She doesn't need to be putting up with this sort of nonsense.'

'Can't you see he's in pain?'

'Look, Miss Spock, I don't care if his heart is broken in ten. He can't be allowed to bully animals and small children as an outlet for his pain. You can kill a kid like Tim with kindness.'

'Oh, how would you know?' Mandy asked miffed.

'No,' Charity said thoughtfully. 'I think you're right, Brett. I'll listen to any suggestions you have. We're losing him. He's drifting further away each day.'

'Fine. He's going to come to work for me every day, and he's going to work until he damn near drops, and he won't have so much time to be sucked down in his self-pity. The alternative is that he leaves the ranch. I can't have a kid like that on the loose around here. Somebody would end up dead. And it would probably be him, if one of my cowhands got a hold of him pulling a brutish, stupid prank like that.'

'You haven't got the authority to be banning guests from the ranch!' Mandy told him.

Brett sighed. 'Charity, would you excuse us for a few minutes? I would like to have a few words in private with the hip-swinging wonder of the world.'

'Charity, if you really love me, you won't walk out that door.'

'Be gentle with her,' Charity told Brett with a wink.

'I don't much subscribe to the gentle school of thought.'

'Poor Mandy,' Charity said, closing the door behind her.

Mandy folded her arms over her chest. 'I'm not afraid of you.'

'Nobody ever said you should be.'

'Then why are you trying to intimidate me?'

He raised a devilish black eyebrow at her. 'I'm not. I can't help it if I'm a foot taller than you and outweigh

you by about sixty pounds. I wouldn't hesitate to use it
to my advantage—but I can't help it.'

'What do you want?'

'Law and order. Peace and quiet. Privacy. Cowhands
unbattered by the rigours of baseball.'

'In other words you want this not be a guest-ranch,'
she said.

'Yes. But failing that, at least in the immediate future,
could we have a well-run guest-ranch?'

'What do you mean?' she gasped. 'I am knocking
myself out to make this an excellent vacation spot for
our guests.'

'Maybe we could have a little less "wiggle, wiggle",
and a lot more fundamentals.'

'Fundamentals?'

'Mrs Abercrombie, this is the way to the baseball
diamond. That sort of thing.'

'Why? Where did Mrs Abercrombie end up?'

'In my living-room. Drinking iced tea.'

'Oh, dear.'

'Don't apologise. Please. Just take five minutes out
of your busy schedule and make a rudimentary map of
the ranch for the guests. Mark my house as a bear den.
Restricted area. Double restricted. No more little old
ladies peering in my window, or young ones primping
on my bed.'

'I am not primping!'

'I think you get the general gist, don't you?'

'Yes.'

'Next. This area is a remote grassland. I feel as fervently about it as those people in your neck of the woods
who chain themselves to trees. Stuff like this makes me

mad. Your guests don't want to make me mad, because when I take a swing, it isn't my hips.'

'Well, then, no root beer and doughnuts for you,' she muttered. He held out the 'stuff' that made him mad. Mandy gazed down at the discarded junk-food bag he thrust into her hands. She felt dreadful about it. She wanted to apologise, but had a feeling she might as well save her breath.

'Three, tell your guests that the wind blows here. Anything they want to keep, they'd better hold down with a rock. Like this.'

He tugged at his front shirt pocket and a red piece of film unravelled from it.

Mandy snatched it from him, balled it up, and tried to jam it in the front pocket of her jeans.

'You wouldn't know who that belongs to, would you?' he asked casually.

'No, I do not.'

'The boys didn't think it was yours.'

'What boys?' she squeaked.

'The cowboys. It blew down to the corrals. Spooked a horse and nearly caused another accident. One accident a day is a pretty bad average, even for you.'

'Well, it's not mine,' she said.

'That's what the boys said too. Wouldn't match your hair, they said. Too big, they said.'

'Too big?' she squawked. 'For heaven's sake, if it was much smaller——' She stopped, flustered by the gauging look in his eyes, and the direction his gaze had moved in.

'I knew it was yours,' he said in a growl.

'I said it wasn't.'

'Don't take up poker.'

'How did you know?' She folded her arms over her chest.

'It caused trouble, and it was red. You might as well have signed it.'

But she knew that wasn't how he knew. He knew because he had held her against him long and hard, and now that moment sizzled between them, a dangerous memory.

'I'll prepare a map,' she said with professional cool, 'and warn the guests about littering...and the wind making off with their possessions.'

'How did you get back to your room?'

'Pardon?'

'When the bathing suit top blew away, how did you get back to your room?'

'Oh. I had a towel.'

'Hmm. You do have a way with a messy situation.'

'Lots of practice.'

For a moment it looked like he might actually smile, but the moment passed and the smile didn't quite materialise.

'Is there anything else I can do to make life more bearable for you?' she asked snippily.

'Yes,' he said.

'What's that?'

'Don't ever wear those jeans again.' He swivelled abruptly on his booted heel and walked away from her, and out the door.

It was the following evening that Mandy found she couldn't sleep. She went down to the kitchen, and heated some milk.

She let out a small shriek when something breathed far too close to her neck. She whirled, and landed right in Felix's arms.

She broke free and eyed him sharply. 'What are you doing?'

'Wanna dancing lesson,' he mumbled, his unfocused eyes on her.

'Absolutely not,' she said sternly. 'How about a coffee, instead?'

'Wanna dancing lesson,' he repeated, coming at her, his arms raised.

Unease was beginning to overshadow her annoyance. She slid away from him. He made a wild grab for her, and caught the lapel of her housecoat. With strength born of desperation she yanked the fabric out of his hands and bolted towards the outside door.

It screeched open before she got there. Brett stood there taking in the scene with narrowed eyes. She had never felt so relieved in her whole life.

She pulled her housecoat primly tight. Was it just because she was so grateful for his presence that he looked so darn good to her?

Dirt clung to his jeans. His shirt was ripped. A smudge of dirt—or was it blood?—covered his right forearm. He looked unimaginably sexy and strong.

'What's going on here?' he asked. His voice was quiet and calm, but the look he gave Felix was killing.

'Nuthin,' Felix said. He slunk from the room.

'Mandy?'

'He's drunk,' she said unsteadily. 'He wanted a midnight dancing lesson.'

'Are you all right?'

'Yes.'

Brett sank into a chair at the formica-topped table, looking thoughtful and perturbed, as he looked at her. He frowned, and she realised she was shaking.

She wanted him to hold her. She turned abruptly back to the stove, afraid her naked need was in her face.

'Are you making cocoa?' he asked hopefully.

'Just warm milk.'

'Ugh.'

'I can make you some cocoa, if you want.'

'I'd be forever indebted to you.'

'Well, that's an opportunity I can't pass up.' He didn't say anything, and she turned and looked at him.

His arms were down on the table pillowing his head.

'Are you all right?'

'I had a sick horse.'

'Is it all right now?'

He lifted his head and looked at her. She read the answer in the bleakness in his eyes.

'What did you do?'

'I had to shoot it. I wish the solution to Felix was that cut and dried.'

'He's just a harmless old drunk,' she said.

'I'll have a talk with him in the morning, Mandy. It might do some good. It might not. Tell me if you have any more problems with him.'

It felt good that he was offering his protection, and bad that one more thing about the guest-ranch was going so terribly that he had to intervene. She looked at the weariness in his face. He did not need more burdens.

'Couldn't you have called a vet? For the horse?'

'The vet's a long way from here. When you've been at this long enough you know when you're wasting his time.'

'I'm sorry.'

'That's the first time I've heard you say that when you didn't do anything.'

'Nincompoop. I'm sorry because you had to shoot the horse. That must have been very unpleasant for you.'

'Yeah. It's been a rougher day than most. How was the kid when he came in?'

'Too exhausted to eat. He just stumbled up to bed, mumbling something about calling the child abuse hotline.'

Brett grunted.

'Maybe you pushed him too hard.'

'Maybe.'

She suspected he conceded not out of conviction but because he was too tired to argue with her.

She set the cocoa down in front of him.

'I don't suppose there's anything to eat around here, is there?'

'I think I could find something. Herman always seems to have lots of leftovers.'

Why did this feel so nice, to be bustling around looking after a tired, hungry man? Her feminist friends would have a fit if they could see her now.

'Thanks,' he said when she set the steaming plate of tacos down in front of him. He dug in. 'This is excellent,' he said.

'I can't take any credit. I just put it in the microwave—which is about the extent of my culinary skill.'

'Are you one of those new-fangled women?' he asked.

She sat down across the table from him. 'What do you mean by new-fangled? Independent? Non-domesticated? Career-orientated?'

'I meant can you cook an egg?' he said drily.

'No.'

He nodded. 'That's what I thought.'

'There are more important things in life,' she told him righteously.

'Like what, Mandy? What's important in life to you?'

'I'm not the philosophical type,' she said wrinkling her nose.

'Give it a try,' he suggested.

'Fine. Important in life. Having fun. Being happy. Harold-the-bear. The Hip-Swinging Hoopla. How's that?'

'It's your life. As long as you're satisfied with it, it's fine with me.' His tired gaze rested with some interest on the little line of black lace that showed above the V of where her housecoat closed.

'Your turn. What's important in life to you?' She pulled her housecoat tight and held it closed at her throat.

He thought for a minute. 'Ending each day knowing I've done the best I was capable of doing.'

She suddenly regretted the quirkiness of her answer. 'You know, Brett,' she said quietly, 'maybe we're not as different as we seem. I know my priorities aren't the same as yours, but believe it or not I do my best every single day. I like giving everything I've got to everything I do, whether I'm teaching kindergarten, or helping people have a good time.'

He finished his food, and sat back for a moment contemplating her. Suddenly, he reached forward and gently took her hand from where it held her housecoat closed.

She stared at him with wide eyes, but made no attempt to stop him when he gently tugged the housecoat open. All the way open.

His eyes were hot as they trailed hungrily over her breasts, enticingly clad in black lace.

'You are the most beautiful woman I have ever seen,' he said, his voice soft and rough.

'T-thank you,' she stammered.

His gaze, hot and lazy, returned to her face. He looked at her for a long time.

Then he scraped back his chair, settled his dark cowboy hat on his head, and went to the door. He paused and looked back at her.

'Too bad about Harold,' he said softly.

He went out into the night.

She sat for a long, long time, her breath coming in strangely ragged gasps.

She was not at all sure if this latest development was an improvement on Brett's thinking of her as a green-eyed monster.

CHAPTER SIX

'MANDY, I will never forget your "rodeo" as long as I live. I've had so much fun.' Charity smiled at her from the steps of the bus.

'Don't go,' Mandy pleaded. 'Stay just one more week.'

Charity laughed. 'You already talked me into an extra week. I've barely seen you in the three weeks I've been here, anyway. You're one busy lady.'

How could Mandy tell her it was just knowing Charity was here, solid as a rock, that helped? She looked at her cousin with mute appeal.

'I miss Matthew,' Charity said softly. 'Matthew misses me...not to mention his son.'

Those soft words created a funny little ache deep in Mandy's soul. What was it like to love someone the way Charity loved Matthew? What was it like to be loved the way Matthew loved Charity?

'Oh, go, then,' Mandy said, 'though it's perfectly disgusting to see a woman of your age and stature in life acting like a lovesick puppy over her man.'

'That's not what you said last summer,' Charity reminded her good-naturedly.

'I've matured,' Mandy proclaimed.

Charity gave a little snort of disbelief, and then grew serious. 'Do you remember what you told me last summer, Mandy?'

'No. Did I say something memorable?'

'You told me I'd been invited to fall in love. You told me I was probably scared to death, but not to run. You told me sometimes a person only gets one invitation to this particular dance, and not to miss my chance.'

'*I* said that?' Mandy's tone was heavy with self-mocking.

'You told me about Gus, and said that you'd missed your chance. But maybe, Mandy, we do get a second invitation, sometimes.'

'Honestly, Charity, I don't know what you're talking about. The only dance I'll be doing this summer is the Hip-swinging Hoopla.'

Charity looked at her intently, then gave her head a small, rueful shake. 'Goodbye, Mandy. I'll miss you. Watch out for Tim for us. Are you sure it's OK to leave him here?'

'It's the only thing to do,' Mandy reassured her.

'Brett did say he really needs him, with Bud's ankle still on the mend, and Tim needs to be needed, right now. Brett was right about plain old hard work and a firm hand, wasn't he?'

Mandy tried not to stiffen up. Brett. Brett, who always seemed to be right. Brett, who was so hardworking he never did come to the baseball games, dances, overnight camp-outs or the rodeos.

The rodeos in particular were a smash hit, and everybody, including *his* cowboys, loved them.

Brett, who was firm with Tim, but also incredibly patient with him, who had worked some sort of miracle on him in several short weeks, but who didn't have so much as the time of day for her.

You are the most beautiful woman I have ever seen. Ha. Sure, buddy, I can tell you find me irresistible.

The morning following that statement Brett had had a talk with Felix, as he had said he would. She could not know the exact words of that 'talk' but the result was that, since that day, Felix avoided her as though she had the plague.

And so did Brett.

Other guests began to come out and she was caught in the whirl of goodbyes—hugs and promises to keep in touch that she knew from experience would never be kept. Not that it mattered—what mattered was how happy these people were. For once, *he* was going to be wrong. This guest-ranch was going to be a success.

'Had the time of my life, Mandy.'

'Can't wait to come back next year.'

'I'm going to come as a paying guest next year.'

Mandy frowned, then forced herself to smile and be casual. 'Mrs Bingle, weren't you a paying guest this year?'

'Oh, no, dear. I didn't think I was the ranch holiday type. James is a dear friend of the family. He insisted I come, and I'm so glad he did.'

'Me too,' Mandy said giving the stout woman, unlikely winner of this week's Most Promising Cowgirl award, a sincere hug. Still, she felt a twinge of distress. How many of the people who had been in and out of here in the last few weeks had actually been paying guests?

'Bye, Mandy.'

'I love you, Mandy.' That from this week's Youngest Cowboy, three-year-old Barney Beaton.

And then she was standing in the dust of the departing bus. She'd have a day and a half to herself, and then the next group would be upon her.

Why did that day and a half yawn ahead of her like a year-long prison term?

She sensed a movement behind her, and turned to see Brett standing in the shadow of the big house porch. Her heart did a little twist inside her chest.

'What is it with you and men?'

'Pardon?'

'Young, old, drunk, sober. They all get a yen for you.'

'I don't know what you mean.' *Not all of them.*

'I just heard Barney proclaim himself.' He came down the steps and stood beside her under the hot Alberta sun.

She laughed. 'Barney proclaims himself quite regularly. He fell in love with me, his pony, the ranch cat, and Herman's special rodeo-flavoured ice-cream.'

'Rodeo-flavoured ice-cream? Sounds a bit scary to me.'

'Well, don't worry about it. Only winning rodeo participants are allowed to have it.'

'From what I understand, everybody wins at one of your rodeos.'

'That's right. Everyone wins. Everyone has a wonderful time. Some people, of course, are averse to having a good time. There's nothing that can be done about that.'

'That's right,' he said solemnly. 'Some people just need to go their own way. It's best to let them.'

'You needn't say that as if any pressure has been put on you, Brett Carpenter, because none has!'

'We were talking about me?' he asked with lazy innocence.

She could feel herself grinding her back teeth together. Another five weeks around this man and she wasn't going to have any back molars left. She forced herself to relax her jaw and remain silent.

'So what prize did you pull down at this week's rodeo?' he asked. 'Reddest hair? Most freckles? Smallest bikini?'

'The categories aren't that ridiculous,' she informed him haughtily.

'Craziest socks?' he breathed.

'Somebody told you!'

'Mandy, every time you make a move over here, I feel the after shock all the way down to the corrals. I hear "Mandy this" or "Mandy that" a minimum of a dozen times a day.'

That news pleased her immeasurably. 'Maybe you need a little shaking up every now and then,' she informed him.

'Yeah,' he said drily. 'I've heard that. That earthquakes are good for people.'

Now he was comparing her to an earthquake! She couldn't stand this man. She deplored him.

So why did she lay awake, night after night, thinking outlaw thoughts about him? Remembering the scrape of his whiskers across her cheeks, the touch of his tongue against her lips?

'You wouldn't want to get stodgy,' she told him sweetly.

'Stodgy,' he choked. 'Stodgy?'

Direct hit, she thought with satisfaction. 'You know, stodgy. Dull, predictable, safe. Never trying anything new or different. I usually associate a little roll of fat with the word, though that doesn't always apply, at least not in the first stages of stodginess.'

He had regained his composure quickly. 'And what do you recommend as a cure for this dread ailment?'

He squinted at her ankles. 'Pink socks? With purple polka-dots on them?'

'It couldn't hurt...for starters.'

'Now that's the part the worries me. For starters. Next thing you know I'd be bungee-jumping from the attic window.'

'With nothing on except a pair of colourful socks,' she couldn't resist elaborating.

He burst out laughing, a good, strong sound, straight from his belly. His teeth were incredibly white, and even.

'Actually,' he told her, becoming stern, 'those socks you're wearing are pretty subdued by your standards, aren't they?'

'That's right,' she said. 'They are.'

'What? Are you sick? It couldn't be first-stage stodginess—not with *you*.'

'I'm going to miss Charity,' she said. 'You don't wear happy socks when you're in mourning.' She had meant it to sound funny, but to her horror a little warble came into her voice.

'Your cousin is a pretty wonderful woman,' he concurred.

Silly as it was, it hurt that Brett could see how wonderful Charity was, but couldn't seem to see one good thing about her.

'Aw, Mandy, don't go and cry on me.'

'I'm not crying,' she said. 'I'm not crying *on* you,' she amended, when a wayward tear slithered down her cheek. She went to brush by him, but a strong arm stopped her.

She looked stubbornly down at the toe of his boot.

He pulled her chin up, and she found green eyes scanning her face with bafflement.

'What's wrong?' he asked.

'I just told you. My best friend in the world just left,' she snapped, slapping his hand away. 'Go nurse a cow.'

'It's more than that,' he guessed softly. 'You pour every bit of yourself into making people happy, into making them laugh, and then suddenly you're all alone. Not even your cousin to confide in.'

She could only hope he didn't guess the kind of confidences she and Charity shared.

'It must be a let-down when they go,' he continued. 'You must feel lonely.'

'Absolutely not,' she said fiercely. 'And I don't need your pity.'

'Pity?' He seemed to find that wildly amusing. 'Pity isn't exactly the feeling you inspire in me, Mandy Marlowe.'

She stared at him. 'Exactly what feeling do I inspire in you, then?'

'Exasperation comes to mind.'

But it wasn't exasperation that had been in his eyes that night that he had opened her housecoat. Not at all. Obviously he was going to pretend that had never happened.

A very wise decision on his part, her rational side felt. But her irrational side had been wildly excited by that moment, and her irrational side had taken over her life. Ever since then, she looked for him. Waited to see him. Waited, caught between fear and excitement, for their next moment together. It hadn't come.

A hood slid smoothly down over his eyes. 'I was just going to see how Tim is doing. I've put him in charge of gentling a filly. Want to come?'

That long-awaited moment had come, after all. But she couldn't let him know, not even guess, how she thought of him, night after restless night, how she wondered, how she waited...

Fight it, she ordered herself. Everybody got a case of the old 'chemical' reaction every now and then. Mature, responsible adults just didn't allow themselves to be ruled by biology rather than their brains. Forget Charity's talk of an invitation, and settle for preservation instead.

'No, I have things to do before guests arrive Monday morning.'

'All right.'

She was offended that he didn't press. Besides, when had she ever behaved like a mature, responsible adult? Come to think of it, nobody had ever accused her of being the brainy type, either.

'Maybe I'll come after all.'

'Suit yourself.' One side of his lip quirked mockingly upwards, and she wondered if she had imagined the warmth of his original invitation.

They walked in silence down to the corrals. It did not feel like the companionable kind of silence books spoke of.

'The filly is quite skittish,' Brett told her, 'so move slowly and speak quietly—if you can.'

'For heaven's sake, I haven't said a word all the way here,' she hissed.

'I know. That's how I could tell you really and truly were in mourning. Only marginally weird socks. No cheerful chatter.'

'Chipmunks chatter cheerfully,' she said, under her breath.

His eyes slid over her. 'Chipmunk. Hmm. I like that. It fits.'

She glared at him. *You are the most beautiful woman I have ever seen*, or *You remind me of a chipmunk*? Come on, Brett Carpenter, which is it going to be?

They moved closer to the corral where Tim had the horse on a long line.

'He's come further than I thought,' Brett said, with satisfaction.

'What is he doing?' she asked quietly.

'He's trying to get the filly so she won't spook so easily. That's why he's got those plastic containers suspended off the stirrups. They've got rocks rattling around in them—to get her used to unusual noises and situations.'

Mandy watched in appreciative silence. Tim was tanned. The pudginess had melted away from his face and his tummy. The wild look of fear and defiance was almost gone from his eyes.

He saw them standing there and grinned a smile of shy pride.

After a while, he approached the young horse, stroking her and talking to her in a low, calm voice.

'Brett, he loves that horse,' she said softly, as they moved away from the corrals.

'Yeah.'

'But isn't it going to hurt when he has to go home? Won't this just be more of the same? Him giving his heart to something, only to lose it?'

'You never lose something you give your heart to.'

'*You*, an expert on hearts?'

'What's so funny about that?' he asked with mock outrage.

'It's not funny exactly. Just...unexpected. I mean you live out here in this lonely country, by yourself.'

'That leaves me this lonely country...and myself to love, I guess,' he said drily.

He did have that easy way of a man totally comfortable with himself, totally content with his own company. The basis of self-esteem was self-love, and lord knew he had enough self-esteem.

'But what's going to happen when he has to leave the filly?' Mandy asked.

'He's going to hurt.'

'Wasn't the idea to get him over his hurt?'

'No. The idea was to let him know that sometimes life hurts, and we survive anyway. The idea was to let him know loving makes us better people, even if it hurts us.'

'How do you know?' she demanded.

'I lost my Dad when I was around twenty. I was a little older than Tim is now, but I don't think I handled it very well,' he said, his voice suddenly soft and unexpectedly serious. 'I loved a girl and I let her go.'

'Why?'

'We were young. She wanted to get married. I was still hurting, still so sure that love meant being hurt. By the time I changed my mind, she'd married someone else.' He smiled cynically. 'Which sort of proved my point.'

'But you haven't given up on Tim.'

'The world doesn't need any more bitter people.'

'You don't strike me as being particularly bitter.'

'Isn't grouchy the same thing?' he asked, sliding her an amused look.

'Not precisely. Is that your entire romantic history?'

'Sorry,' he said drily. 'I thought you knew by now I'm not very entertaining.'

'I didn't mean it as a put-down,' she said hastily. 'I was just surprised. You're a very attractive man.' The most beautiful man I've ever seen, if I was going to be honest about it. Which she was not.

'Not to cows, though you've suggested otherwise on more than one occasion. Now your love-life is probably entertaining. Jealous boyfriends and wealthy playboys and...'

She should play it safe. Given the sizzling attraction she felt for this silent, strong cowboy, she should let him believe that.

But when had a Marlowe, save for Charity, the family black sheep, ever played it safe? Even Charity had been good for a few surprises last summer when she and Matthew had rather stormily wooed one another.

'I'm not exactly getting movie offers on the thrilling romances that don't fill my life.'

'Come on. What about Harry?' Despite his casual tone, she sensed what she said next was very important.

Though it was still somewhat embarrassing to say it.

'He's a teddy-bear,' she mumbled.

'What?'

'Harold's a teddy-bear,' she said. 'You know, fake fur and button eyes.'

His eyes locked with hers, and for one smoldering moment she thought he was going to grab her and kiss the living daylights out of her.

Instead, he threw back his head and laughed. 'You are the most outrageous person I've ever met.'

You are the most beautiful woman I have ever seen. When were they going to get to that part?

'You've been sheltered,' she told him.

The laughter died in his eyes. 'What about my boss?'

'James and I are just friends,' she said uncertainly.

'For now?' he guessed, hearing the uncertainty.

She looked up at him. Looked at the strong lines of his face, the clean line of his mouth, the colour of his eyes.

She wanted to say, Make me a better offer. She didn't.

'I loved somebody once, too, you know,' she heard herself saying.

'Did you? What happened to happily ever after?'

'He died.' She tilted her chin fiercely at him, daring him to pity her.

'I'm sorry,' he said, his voice very soft, and his eyes very gentle. 'That must have been very hard.'

'It was.' Harder than anyone could ever know. 'I suppose I should go back to the house,' she said, feeling suddenly vulnerable and open.

'I suppose,' he said.

'OK, then. Bye.'

'Goodbye.'

She turned and walked away.

'Mandy?'

She turned back to him, much too quickly. 'Yes?'

'Would you like to go for a ride with me tomorrow?'

'Yes!' Oh, how she wanted to grab back that impulsive yes, and say a more demure, 'I'll think about it.'

'There's a buffalo jump about a two-hour ride from here. It might make an interesting day-trip for your guests to visit it next week.'

She tried to get behind his eyes. She couldn't. Surely he wasn't just asking her because it was a point of interest that she as the ranch entertainment director should be familiar with?

No, there was more to it than that. Brett didn't even like the guests.

Pity? Because she was lonely, and because in a moment of unguarded trust she had let him know something about her past that very few people knew?

No. It was not pity that lit that strong, handsome face, as if the sun shone from within him.

With her heart skipping happily, and her every ounce of will focused on not allowing her feet to do the same, she walked back up towards the big house.

She stopped. 'What time?' she called back to him.

'Eight.' He grinned at her. It was a grin that said her eagerness was not very well masked at all.

Why had she told him he was attractive? That was a terrible weapon to give a man like that.

She wondered if she had just made a big mistake.

She wondered why she didn't care.

That night she was exhausted but couldn't sleep. Her room was a catastrophe. She had tried on everything she owned at least once, searching for the perfect look. Gorgeous, but utterly casual. She didn't want him to know she'd made an effort to look gorgeous, after all.

About midnight she had settled on an ivory camisole, underneath a black Western shirt that she would leave mostly unbuttoned, and those sinful jeans he'd asked her never to wear again.

Then she'd gone to bed, too exhausted and excited to even put the discards away.

By two she still wasn't sleeping.

Of course, she thought, for the hundredth time, he's going to kiss me.

They were going to be alone together for the first time since that night in the kitchen.

And she knew it was going to be deliciously dangerous. So did he. Didn't he?

Was that why he had avoided her for all this time? Because of the danger that sizzled like summer heat in the air between them?

And why, now, had he given in?

And why was she? Despite Charity's none-too-subtle hinting that she should see where this attraction to Brett might lead, she already knew.

Precisely nowhere. They were too different, she and that silent, puzzling cowboy. He was far too stern and serious. His lifestyle and hers couldn't be reconciled in a million years.

So why had she said yes, then, to an encounter that seemed destined to heat up, but never bake?

She sighed. It was her weakness she supposed. An addiction to excitement. And he was an exciting man.

Even if he never tried anything new as long as he lived, he would still be an exciting man.

It was *in* him. In the powerful, sensual way he moved, and in the slow, soft way his words scraped across her nerve-endings and the smoky way his jade-shaded eyes could set her libido on fire.

Even Charity, who was more conservative than most, had told her not to run away from these feelings that baffling man was stirring up in her. Physical feelings.

But why not? Why not have a summer, one sizzling summer, where she followed her heart where it led?

She hoped he would kiss her ears.

Eight o'clock came. And then eight-thirty. He realised the little chit wasn't coming.

It hadn't been the best idea, anyway. Downright stupid, if he thought about it. Which he should have done before he opened his mouth.

He'd spent nearly three weeks staying out of her clutches.

But her cousin had been right.

Mandy Marlowe had put a spell on him. He thought about her green eyes with ridiculous frequency. And about her red bikini top. And especially about the way she had looked in black lace.

He thought about her laughing, and doing that foolish dance.

Mostly when he thought about her he knew damn well she was trouble, and he did what any smart man would do.

He ran the other way.

But yesterday those diamond tears glittering in those big eyes had caught him off guard. Completely off guard. It hadn't helped finding out she didn't have a boyfriend named Harold.

It hadn't helped finding out she wasn't at all committed to James Snow-Pollington.

It hadn't helped finding out that underneath all that effervescent energy was a woman whose man had died, who held some secret sorrow to her heart.

No, all those things had added up, and he had not behaved sensibly. He had, in fact, ruined his investment in a stodgy future completely.

He knew they couldn't go for a ride alone together without getting in all kinds of trouble. He knew that. He knew he should feel grateful that she hadn't come.

He looked at the two saddled horses. He'd just take the saddle off Dixie, and go for a ride himself. That was what he'd do.

'Like hell,' he said under his breath, and started towards the big house.

'Go away,' Mandy mumbled, the loud banging on her door registering somewhere in her sleep-clogged brain.

The banging persisted. She pulled her pillow over her head.

The door crashed open, and the wakeful state she'd been struggling against was on her abruptly.

She sat up, her heart pounding, and focused.

'Oh,' she flopped back down, closed her eyes, and put a hand over her palpitating heart. 'It's just you.'

Her eyes snapped back open, and she tugged frantically at a sheet to cover the lacy teddy she slept in. 'You! What are you doing in my room?'

'You and I made a date for eight. I might be *just* a cowboy, but I think I deserved the courtesy of a cancellation, if you changed your mind.'

And then she remembered. Her eyes flew to her little bedside clock. It was nearly nine o'clock.

Forgetting modesty, she sat up on one elbow and gave the clock a hearty smack. The alarm immediately started to ring.

'Darn thing,' she muttered. 'It doesn't work right.' She gave it a few more smacks, for good measure, and then turned back to Brett.

'How do you function in day-to-day life?' he asked, with dry interest.

'I'm sorry.'

The anger had dissipated from his face and he was looking at her with reluctant amusement.

'Please, don't apologise, Mandy. It always makes me wonder what I'm in for.' His eyes roved around the room. 'Not much of a housekeeper, are you?'

'I wasn't expecting company,' she said indignantly. After all, it was really his fault her room looked like this. Partly his fault. 'I can be ready in ten minutes. Honest.'

He looked at his watch. 'Ten minutes,' he agreed, without moving.

'Well, you have to leave.'

'Oh, darn.'

She picked up something and threw it at him.

He caught it out of mid-air, and studied it. 'Harold, I presume.'

'Where *are* my manners? Harold, Brett. Brett, Harold. Now, out.'

He still didn't move. Then he took one long step forward, and gazed down at her for a long second. He leaned over and kissed her on her cheek.

His face was very close to hers. They stared at each other. He straightened.

'You look beautiful in the morning,' he said gruffly.

It hung in the air between them. TROUBLE in capital letters.

'I think I should have left without you,' he said softly.

'I think I should roll over and go back to sleep,' she said, just as softly.

'See you in ten minutes.'

'Five.'

There was nothing romantic about horseback riding, Mandy decided, even though the scenery around them was certainly dramatic—grasslands rolling and undu-

lating, with the sharp forbidding peaks of the Rocky
Mountains not too distant in the west. She was not a
good rider, and her attention pretty much had to stay
focused on staying in the saddle.

Which was just as well. There was no telling what
might happen if her attention strayed—say, to the way
his jeans fitted.

She held the reins in one hand, and kept the other
firmly on the saddle horn, even though Brett had
suggested it wasn't necessary.

The man looked as if he'd been born in the saddle.
How did he know what was necessary for a greenhorn?

She had been on many of the trail rides Blair led, but
they had not prepared her for this. Brett either liked to
travel at a bone-jarring trot or liked torturing people.
His horse had longer legs and a quicker pace than hers,
and he had moved slightly ahead of her, which pre-
cluded their even chatting.

It seemed like they had been riding for a very long
time and it was beginning to get very warm out.

The blush of being told she was beautiful this morning
was fast fading from her cheeks.

'Black might have been a poor choice of colour,' he
said, reining in the impatient horse he rode, and making
it prance beside hers.

'You mean your horse?' she asked.

'No. I meant your shirt. It'll really attract the heat.'

'Oh. My shirt.' *Black looks glorious with my hair, you
boob.*

'Is this ride going to be a little too ambitious for you?'
he asked, regarding her critically.

*Did that mean he was thinking of taking her
home already?*

'Oh, no,' she said. 'I'm fine.' As long as we're nearly there.

'Are you sure? The buffalo jump is about an hour from here. Let me know if it's too much.'

'Sure.'

'I'd like to run this big guy for a while. He's too full of spit and vinegar.'

'Oh, sure. Whatever you want.'

Unfortunately, when his mount plunged ahead, hers did too. She locked on to the saddle-horn and suffered while the horse bounced her all over the place.

It seemed like about a hundred miles before he decided to slow down.

'Wasn't that great?' he said. 'There's nothing like the wind in your hair, is there?'

She could only guess what the wind had done to her hair.

'We live in two different worlds, don't we? A million miles apart.'

'What?' he asked, pulling his horse in abruptly. 'What do you mean?'

'I mean I have sore knees. And sore thighs. And a sore back. Brett, I have a sore bum.'

'Why didn't you say so? Mandy, I asked you if you were OK.'

'I didn't want you to think I was a quitter.'

'I already know you're no quitter.'

'And I wanted you to think I was the hardy, horsy type.'

'Why?'

'I wanted you to like me.'

He looked stunned. 'You wanted me to like you? Why? What plans do you have for the ranch now?'

'I don't have any plans for your stinking ranch!'

'For me?' he said suspiciously.

'See? You always think the worst of me.'

'Do I?'

'I just don't understand why you don't like me. Damn it, you stubborn old cowboy, I'm nice!'

'I've never said I didn't like you,' he said quietly. He had guided them into a stand of cottonwoods that lined a small creek. He stopped his horse, and got smoothly from the saddle.

He came over and helped her off her own mount. Her knees buckled and she lurched against him.

His arms came around her. 'Damn you, Mandy, it's not that I don't like you. I like you too damn much.'

'You do?'

'What did you think I asked you to come out here for? I'm intrigued by you. I want to get to know you better.'

'Really?'

'Well, what did you think?'

'I thought you liked . . . kissing me.'

'Well, I won't deny that.'

'I thought maybe you were going to lay me down on a blanket, way out in the middle of nowhere, and kiss me all over.'

'I did bring a blanket,' he said thickly.

'I was even kind of hoping that's what you had planned.'

'Really?' he said hoarsely.

'But, Brett, I can't. We can't.'

'We can't?'

'I've never hurt like this in my life,' she moaned, sinking down pathetically under a tree. 'I don't think I'm going to be able to ride back.'

'You've got to ride back,' he said.

'Well, I can't.'

'Mandy——' he sank down beside her, and tugged at one of her curls '—why do I have this funny feeling that liking you and disliking you are about the same exasperating experience?'

'Sor——'

'Don't,' he whispered, his mouth very close to hers. 'Tell me, do your lips hurt?'

'No. They are the one part of my anatomy that seems to have been spared.'

He kissed her gently, thoroughly, stealing the very breath from her lungs.

'Brett,' she whispered. 'Come to think of it, my ears don't hurt, either.'

CHAPTER SEVEN

'WE'RE going to have to take your jeans off.' They were words that had entered his dreams on and off in the last three weeks.

He should have known that with Mandy nothing was going to be a dream. Not even taking off her jeans.

'I'm so embarrassed,' she said.

'I take the blame entirely. I should have assessed your riding skills before we even left.'

Unfortunately, he had been rather preoccupied. He had never seen a woman look as glorious as Mandy Marlowe had looked when he had burst into her bedroom.

Her red curls had been scattered across her pillow, and her cheeks had been pink with sleep. Her lashes were so long they cast shadows on her cheeks.

She had been wearing a delicate little something that looked as if it was constructed out of spider webs, her skin smooth and creamy underneath it, her breasts full and round where they pressed into its scant protection.

He'd given into the temptation to kiss her, which was how they had landed in this predicament. His mind had been on kisses, and he'd been trying fervently to get it to move somewhere else. Which was pretty bloody difficult with her riding along behind him, with that little ivory camisole peeking out of her shirt at him, and those little lips forming perfect kissable bows.

He'd tried to ignore her, in an effort to get the worst of his animal instincts under control. He'd succeeded only in ignoring her. The animal instincts had raged on unabated.

But he was paying the price now for both his negligence and his raging desire.

'Brett,' she'd whispered. 'Come to think of it, my ears don't hurt either.' A feeling close to bliss had enveloped him. It was all the invitation he'd needed. He'd been kissing her with growing hunger, his hands exploring with ragged delight when her sharp cry of pain had stopped him.

'You can't touch me there,' she'd said. 'It's too painful.'

And then he'd known he was going to have to have a look at the injuries.

He undid the snap on her jeans, saying a little prayer for control.

'Let's have a look at the damage,' he said, congratulating himself on his nice even tone.

'Brett, this is horrible.'

It's not exactly what I imagined, either. 'Don't worry about it.'

As gently as he could he slid the jeans over the fullness of her hips. Her panties were ivory silk, the front a fascinating V, shaped in lace.

He drew in a ragged breath, and tugged the jeans off.

The delicate skin of her inner thighs was already beginning to bruise.

'Aw, Mandy, why didn't you say something?'

'I bruise easily,' she said, 'I'm sure it looks worse than it feels.'

He touched the bruise with a finger and she groaned. 'I'm sure it doesn't,' he muttered. He checked the rest of her legs. The skin on the inside of her knees was rubbed raw.

He took a deep, grim breath. 'This is my fault. I thought you'd been riding every day. Actually, I didn't think nearly enough. I've been riding as long as I've been walking. It just never occurred to me how tender someone could be.'

'It's not your fault at all, Brett. I behaved foolishly. I should have told you as soon as I started to get uncomfortable. I just wanted so badly to measure up...for once.'

That felt like a thrust to the heart. Had he been that nasty to her, that she felt like she had to measure up? He knew he had been.

'Mandy, let's try sitting you in the creek for a bit. We'll have a rest, and the lunch I brought, and maybe in an hour or so...' His voice trailed off dubiously.

How the hell was he going to get her back to the ranch? He was probably going to have to take her in his lap. There was no way she was going to be able to sit astride her mount. But it would still be a painful, long ride for her.

He set her in the creek. It was only a few inches deep, and she squealed when the cold water rushed over her.

To his dismay, the panties that were temptation itself to begin with turned transparent in the water.

She splashed him. 'Quit looking so grim.'

He tried to smile. He thought he probably smiled like the grinch who stole Christmas.

'I feel much better now,' she said a few minutes later. Using his shoulder to anchor herself, she pulled herself up.

He sucked in his breath, as he looked at her, those shapely legs beaded with water, her filmy panties clinging to her.

He stood up abruptly, whipped off his shirt, and knotted it around her waist.

'Let's eat,' he said. He wondered how the hell he was going to survive.

Hadn't he wondered that from the very start? How the hell was he going to survive Mandy Marlowe?

'So, tell me about you,' Mandy asked him, nibbling without much interest on a chicken leg. Brett looked grim and remote.

And unbearably sexy without his shirt on. His naked chest was a light golden brown, perfect and masculine in every way. She wanted to run her fingers along it, and then her lips and then her tongue.

She took another bite of her chicken.

'Me? I don't think there's much to tell.'

'Oh, sure there is. You can tell me about growing up on a ranch, and the girl you loved long ago, and the work you do now.'

He seemed to relax slightly. It turned out he had grown up on this ranch. His father had been the manager of it, and his grandfather before that. He told her about ranch Christmases, and his first pony, and the time a bull had chased him up a skinny little aspen tree.

The grim look was receding from his face.

'And what about the girl you loved?' Mandy asked, handing him a chocolate chip cookie from the lunch pack he'd produced. Her fingertips touched his, and lingered.

She pulled them hastily away. There was no sense teasing ... herself or him.

The grim look was back on his face.

'It was a long time ago, and there isn't much to tell. She lived on the ranch next door. She was the closest neighbour of my age. We hung around together. Lord, that girl could ride.'

Mandy tugged his shirt down over the evidence of her own poor riding skills.

His eyes followed the movement. He swallowed and looked at the sky. The grim look was not going away.

'Essentially we grew up together. Played, fought, went to school, worked. As we got older we just naturally fell into a relationship.'

'But it didn't go anywhere?'

'Everybody thought it would. There was a lot of pressure put on us, as I recall. But we were very young. I didn't want to get married and she did. In the end, she moved away. Married a doctor in Calgary. Her parents sold out a few years ago, and she hasn't been back this way.

'Coincidentally, though, that girl—woman now—is scheduled to be one of the ranch's guests. Next week, I think.' The grim look had disappeared from his face.

Mandy felt the funniest little squeeze in the pit of her stomach. 'Really? Isn't that odd?'

But she didn't think it was odd at all. If she'd left a man like Brett behind, she was sure she'd be back some day. He wasn't the kind of man you would get out of your system.

'What's her name?' Deliberately she slid a leg out from underneath his shirt.

'Lillian. Lillian Merriweather now.' He didn't look away from his determined study of the cloud formations.

'Did you ever feel sorry that you didn't marry her?'

'I guess I've wondered from time to time if it was a mistake to let her go. Even though we're sort of in the back of beyond here, I have occasionally been involved with other women. And it's true, I have compared them to her.

'She was the easiest person I've ever been around. We were very compatible. You'd probably think she was sober-sided, but she knew this life and what it asks of people. She was very mature, even back then.'

Mandy decided not to ask him if he'd ever compared her to Lillian. She was not sure she'd compare very favourably to someone like that. She tucked her leg back under his shirt.

'Don't you ever wish for kids or anything?' Mandy asked.

'Wishing *is* for kids,' he told her, with a smile that was slightly sad, and said more than his answer had. 'And what about you, Mandy Marlowe, do you have some maternal longing ticking away inside of you?'

'My maternal longings are pretty much satisfied by twenty-odd kindergarten kids. I mean, some day I plan to have children of my own, when the time is right.'

'Yeah. That's what I thought, too. But the time was never right. Maybe if you wait for everything to be just perfect, it never is.' He regarded her intently. 'Did I say something wrong?'

'No. No, of course not.'

'Do you want to tell me about him?'

She smiled at his perception. 'Yes, I do. I'm not sure why, but I do. His name was Gus. He was the handyman at the lodge I usually work at.'

'Anpetuwi.'

She felt surprised that he remembered. 'That's right. Anyway, he was quite a bit older than me.'

'How much?'

'Ten years.'

'Much too old for you,' he muttered.

She realised it was a blessing that the physical side had been shut down before it got away from them. It might have convinced them both to get into something they just weren't ready for—something that might prove absolutely disastrous.

'Anyway, he wasn't a dream man or anything like that, you know? He was really homely and not a snazzy dresser or anything. But, oh, he made me laugh. Usually I'm the one making people laugh, but Gus could really tickle my funny bone. And I could talk to him like no one I had ever talked to. Not that I have much difficulty talking, but with Gus I could say how I really felt. I guess I felt safe being completely me with him. I didn't do the song and dance I sometimes do when I'm not very sure of myself. Gus was an extremely humble man, and very wise. I loved him and I knew I loved him.

'He asked me to marry him and my heart said yes, this is the one. Gus is it. But you talked before about sort of waiting for perfection, and I'm ashamed to say that's what I chose to do. I wanted to look for a fairy-tale. I thought maybe I should love somebody younger and more handsome and with a little more stature in the world. I thought I could look around a bit more, and that Gus would always be there if I changed my mind.

'I was wrong. I was so wrong.' She was crying quietly, and Brett shifted over, and put his arm around her shoulder. He tucked her head into his chest. He said nothing, but the gentleness of his hand stroking her hair said more about him than words could have said anyway.

'I'm sorry,' she sniffed.

'Mandy,' he said softly, 'you use apologies inappropriately.'

She giggled shakily.

'Thank you for telling me about him, and don't be so hard on yourself. We can never know whether the decisions we've made are right or wrong. We just don't have the big picture.'

'What do you mean?'

'If you'd married Gus,' he said softly, his eyes intent on her face, 'you would have never met me. And you were destined to meet me, Mandy Marlowe.'

'I was?' she breathed. Did he think, then, there was something else between them besides these physical feelings? Did he think destiny was at work in their lives? Did he think they were star-crossed——

'Oh, sure. I'd grown much too complacent. I needed an earthquake or two in my life.'

She gave him a smart smack on the shoulder with her fist. His tone had become teasing, but she was sure she would never forget the look in his eyes when he'd said those words.

If you'd married Gus, you would have never met me.

'How are your legs feeling now?' His hand dropped from her hair, and he put her away from his shoulder.

'I'll live.'

'You'll live, but by the time we get back, you may wish that you weren't going to. We'd better go soon be-

cause we'll have to take it really slow and easy on the
way back. I'm going to put you on my horse in front
of me.'

She should have felt relieved, but it seemed like that
was a long way to go with Brett's big arms around her,
his chest behind her. Hours of sweet torture.

'Here. Put these back on.' He handed her her jeans
and turned his back to her.

She slipped his shirt from around her waist, and put
on her jeans. Briefly, she gave into the temptation to
hold the shirt to her nose before she returned it to him.

He stirred volcanic passions in her.

She was stunned by her reaction to this man.

And right now she was helpless to do anything about
it. The trip home was going to be torture in more ways
than one.

She looked at his troubled face.

And not just for her.

He pulled the shirt on, buttoned it, tucked it into his
trousers. She did not have the modesty to turn away from
him as he had from her.

He got on his horse, reached down, grasped her under
the armpits and swung her across his saddle. He led the
other horse.

It was a pure form of joy, being snuggled up to him
like this, she thought, her head resting against his
shoulder, the strong band of his arm supporting her back
and his hand resting lightly on her midriff.

She looked up into the green of his eyes. He looked
down at her and smiled.

She felt drowsy and happy. She felt as if she didn't
care about the future. This moment, this magic moment
with Brett was enough.

She awoke to a sound she thought was thunder. 'Brett?'

His arm was too tight around her. She looked into his face, and saw the tight line of strain around his lips.

The noise wasn't stopping, but growing louder and louder, like the roar of a 747 rumbling down the tarmac.

'Hang on, Mandy!' he called over the noise. 'Don't panic.'

Panic? What on earth was he talking about? She twisted in his arms and her mouth fell open.

They were directly in the path of a dark, lunging mass of cattle. The cattle were wild-eyed, snorting and bellowing.

'Stampede,' she heard him say. He let go of the horse he was leading, and then the dust was all around them, clogging her eyes and her throat and her nose. She clung to him with raw terror, as the horse lunged beneath them.

His horse was charging along with cattle now, caught in the middle of this maelstrom, being jostled on all sides as the panicked herd streamed around them.

Above the relentless thunder of pounding hooves, she could hear the desperate shouts of men, see dimly the shapes of cowboys riding the outside of the herd, trying to bring it under control.

She pressed her nose into the hardness of Brett's chest, trying to escape the dust that was choking her.

She could feel the steady vibration of that strong heart beating, the tension in his skin, the powerful coiling of muscles, as he fought for control of his mount, fought to keep them both in the saddle.

And then it was over, the thunder moving past them, the dust clearing around them. They were left behind by the crazed herd.

She lifted her nose from his chest, and looked into the clear jade of his eyes. His face was streaked with dirt and dust and sweat.

He peered down at her, his arms still tight around her. 'Are you all right?'

'Yes,' she said shakily. 'I think so. Are you?'

'Yes.' His grip loosened on her, and he touched her cheek with a big thumb.

'My lips remain miraculously uninjured,' she whispered.

He lowered his own lips to hers. 'Miraculous,' he agreed. She could taste the dust in his mouth.

Their lips celebrated the miracle of life.

Suddenly his head jerked away from hers.

'What?'

He placed a finger on her lips, and cocked his head, listening to a sound she could not hear over the stampede of her own heart beat. She nuzzled his finger.

'Son-of-a-bitch,' he said under his breath.

She quit nibbling his finger and listened. For a moment she heard nothing. Then she heard the steady wop-wop-wop of helicopter blades cutting the air.

'But who would be so stupid?' she demanded.

Brett's eyes were fixed on the sky. In a moment the helicopter came into view.

'Guess,' he said tersely.

'Guess? I don't know anybody with a helicopter.'

The machine was hovering above them. Brett's horse danced nervously but he held it firmly in check.

The helicopter began to descend. It landed not far from them, whoever was in it apparently insensitive to what the noise of the machine was doing to the already high-strung horse.

'Who the hell is that?' she charged with fury. 'How could anybody be so dim?'

The arms that had held her so safe slipped from around her waist. She looked at him questioningly, but his eyes were on the helicopter. He let her slide to the ground.

Her body had stiffened up again, and she had to grab one of the stirrups to keep from falling. Pain shot through her limbs.

A figure emerged from the helicopter, crouched low, and came towards them. Then he straightened.

'James!' She stared at him with disbelief.

She turned quickly to look at Brett.

Whatever he was thinking was not apparent in the remote set of his face.

'Mandy,' James came up to her. It looked like he was going to embrace her but then he stopped short. 'My God, girl, you look as if you've been dragged through a mud puddle backwards.'

Mandy couldn't miss the angry snort from the man mounted on the horse behind her.

'J-James,' she stammered, 'What on earth are you doing here?'

'I've been looking all over for you,' he cried over the steady noise of the helicopter.

Her mouth fell open. Indirectly, she was the cause of this disaster? How could James be such an idiot?

He was grinning at her with endearing boyish charm. She realised he either had no idea what he had done— or if he did no idea of the seriousness of it.

She sensed Brett shift impatiently in the saddle. The movement drew James's attention away from her. 'Brett, old chap, how are you?'

'I've been better.'

'Sorry, can't hear you. We'll chat when you get back to the ranch.'

Mandy shifted uncomfortably to look at Brett. His gaze was not on James, but on her.

'Count on that,' Brett said, eyes as cold as chips of green ice moving to James and then drifting back to her face. One dark eyebrow went up.

Mandy pulled away from James's hand that rested lightly on her shoulder.

With a sardonic grin, Brett tipped his hat to her, wheeled the big horse he rode and galloped away.

'What were you doing riding with Brett, anyway, love? Is there a shortage of horses around here all of a sudden?'

'It's a long story.' She gestured at the helicopter, indicating she didn't want to yell above it. He offered her his arm, and she linked her arm through it and limped beside him back towards the chopper.

The helicopter took off. When she looked out the window, she could see Brett, galloping hell-for-leather over the open grasslands. He looked as if he came from a different time. A different world. He looked strong, independent, utterly free.

He didn't look up as they passed over him. He did not wave goodbye.

She didn't say a word to James in the helicopter. She was glad the noise of the contraption gave her an excuse for not speaking. Then they were at the house. That infernal racket finally stopped.

And he was standing there just as she remembered him, tall and lanky, his blue eyes lazy and laughter-filled on her face.

'So are you happy to see me?'

She felt tired and confused. She felt sore in places she didn't know she had. She felt she'd betrayed Brett by coming back with James, even though the decision had been made by Brett.

'Surprised,' she offered.

'You look an absolute fright. Why don't you go get cleaned up and then we'll have a nice reunion? How are the liquor stocks? I could use a drink.'

The liquor stocks were somewhat depleted by Felix, she was sure. And *he* could use a drink?

It was on the tip of her tongue to tell him his irresponsibility had nearly killed her and Brett.

He reached out and gave her nose an affectionate little tweak. 'I've missed you. You have a way of haunting a man, Mandy Marlowe, did you know that?'

The angry words died in her throat.

He was handsome, wealthy, and charming. But somehow the fact that he was haunted by her, rather than flattering her, filled her with an odd sense of dread.

She dragged herself up the stairs to her room. She wished she never had to come back down them.

She desperately needed a bath, but she flopped down on her bed, and studied her ceiling. It was ridiculously romantic that James had been flying around the ranch in a helicopter searching for her. She was well aware that three weeks ago his flair for the grand gesture had seemed more exciting than it did now. For some reason, today, she could see the immaturity in it.

Had she changed that much in three weeks?

Of course, James was a city-slicker, just as she was. It wasn't as if he'd stampeded the cattle on purpose. He didn't even seem aware that he'd done it.

She'd been given a fright, but really it wasn't her job to take James to task for what had been a simple error. Technically he was her boss. You didn't just give your boss what for.

Or at least she didn't. She had a feeling that James's position was not going to protect him for the wrath of Brett.

They were so different these two men. As different as night and day. How did they manage to get along at all?

Brett had found the herd, now grazing quietly. Nobody had been injured, and he had recaptured Dixie.

By the time he got back to the ranch his fury had chilled within him.

He should have known. She was that kind of woman. A woman men crossed continents to see. A woman a man would search for with a helicopter...or a camel, if it came to that. A woman who made a man lose any common sense he possessed.

Not that James Snow-Pollington possessed much to begin with, he thought with a sigh.

But he did. What was his excuse for getting involved with Mandy Marlowe when he'd known, right from that first moment he'd laid eyes on her, that it would be about the craziest thing a man could do?

CHAPTER EIGHT

WHEN Mandy awoke her room was in deep shadow. How long had she slept? She moved to look at her clock, and moaned. There was not a place on her body that did not hurt.

Except her lips, she thought, and touched them with a whimsical smile.

It crept into her mind that James was here, and that she had agreed to clean up and meet him for a drink. That had been two hours ago. With a sigh, she sat up, got out of bed and took a few wobbly steps over to her mirror.

She looked a sight, her face streaked with grime, and her hair dirty and stringy, her clothes beyond repair.

Carefully, she stripped them off and went into the bath. She ran the water very hot and was very liberal with the bubbles. She got in and, despite the fact she was running very late, gave in to the temptation of a good long soak.

Her aching body felt quite a bit better as she stepped out of the tub. She dried off and threw on the little wrap she kept behind the door. The wrap, white satin, with a dragon embroidered on the back, was very short, and ended at mid-thigh.

She had just taken a comb to the hopeless tangle of her hair when a knock came at the door.

She went and stood behind it, opened it and then tipped her head around. 'Yes?'

James was standing in the hallway, precariously balancing a tray with a chilled bottle of champagne and two fluted glasses.

'Let me in before I lose the works,' he said.

She opened the door, and he scurried past her, setting the tray down on her bedside table and sinking on to the bed.

'Whew. That was a close call. I guess I'm not too suited to being a waiter.' His eyes scanned her, and he whistled. 'That's an improvement.' His eyes lingered appreciatively on her legs, and then he frowned.

Self-consciously she tried to pull the short dressing-gown down further.

He came up off the bed, and bent and looked at her legs.

'James!'

'I've seen you in a bikini, for heaven's sake. What on earth happened to your legs?'

She looked down. Sure enough the bruises were darkening to a nice ghoulish shade of green.

'I bruise easily,' she muttered.

'Well, all right, but you bruise easily doing what?'

'Riding.'

'Did this happen today?'

'Well, yes, but——'

'I would expect Brett to take better care of you than that, for God's sake. What was the man thinking of? That you were one of his made-of-leather hands?'

'It's really got nothing to do with Brett. It was my own fault.'

'What were you doing with Brett, anyway?'

Something in James's voice drew her up short, and warned her to answer this question carefully.

'He said there was a buffalo jump near here that might be of interest to the guests.'

James put his arms around her and he pulled her to him. 'I was jealous,' he said.

She wedged her arms up between them. 'How about that champagne?' she asked, a little desperately.

He broke away from her immediately. 'Terrific idea.' He fetched the bottle and struggled with the cork. It finally flew off and imbedded itself in the ceiling.

He poured the glasses, and turned and handed her one.

'To us,' he said softly.

She stared at him. 'Uh——'

There was a sharp knock on the door.

'Oh, hell,' James said. He went and yanked on the door.

Felix stood there. His eyes flitted in, rested on her with oily appreciation, and then moved nervously back to James.

'Well, what, man?' James roared.

'Mr Carpenter is here, sir. He says he wants to see you.'

'Not now,' James said impatiently.

Felix shifted his weight, obviously weighing which man he was more afraid of. 'He said he wanted to see you now. He was not exactly polite about it, sir.'

'Oh, all right. Go and tell him I'll be there in a minute.' He turned apologetically back to Mandy. 'Our reunion gets postponed again. Carpenter said in his telegram that he had some fairly important business to discuss with me.'

She registered that James wasn't just here to see her as he had implied. And she registered that it was a relief

that he hadn't come all this way just to see her. She had
nothing to offer James, and she wasn't quite sure how
to tell him that.

'Wait right here. Don't move a muscle. I'll be back
in five minutes.'

She smiled uneasily at him.

He winked at her. 'And by the way, Mandy, you are
a worse housekeeper than I am.'

The door had not been closed a full second before she
slammed home the lock, threw off her housecoat, and
jammed her aching limbs into some clean, if faintly
wrinkled clothes. She yanked a comb through the wet
tangle of her hair, and then, with only the quickest look
in the mirror, she picked up the champagne and the
glasses and put them back on the tray.

There was no way she was going to sit in a state of
undress and sip champagne on her bed with Lord James
Snow-Pollington.

With her tongue caught between her teeth she ma-
noeuvred out of her room and down the hall with the
tray.

A safe place, she thought, would be the dining-room.
She squinted at the sloshing glasses. No doubt they'd be
empty by the time she got down a flight of stairs with
them.

She was just shuffling past the office when the door
was flung open, and Brett came out. He crashed right
into her.

The glasses shattered as soon as they hit the floor. The
bottle landed with a clank and the champagne oozed out
around their feet.

Brett grabbed her shoulders to steady her, and then
let her go abruptly.

He hadn't changed yet and he looked tired, dirty…and angry.

She sucked in her breath, as his sparking eyes took in the scene with cool displeasure. The downward creases around his mouth deepened.

'Would you like to join James and me for a drink?' she said wanting desperately to erase the wrong conclusions that glared so accusingly at her from his eyes.

'No, thanks,' he said tightly.

'Brett——' She blocked his path.

'He's more your type, lady,' he said in a low growl, pushing her out of his way with barely leashed savagery.

She stood there, in a puddle of champagne, watching him go, the scent of a hard-working man lingering in the air behind him, and making her think renegade thoughts of Brett Carpenter in a bubble bath.

'Good lord, love, what happened here?' James appeared in the office doorway.

'I dropped the damn stuff, OK?'

'Well, don't bite my head off. I'll get you a straw if the Dom Perignon means that much to you.'

He smiled engagingly at her. She smiled weakly back.

'I'll rustle up another bottle of wine,' he said, using what he assumed was ranch vernacular with obvious enjoyment, 'and we'll get some dinner. All right?'

But it felt like nothing was going to be all right, again.

'The cook doesn't work weekends, but I'm sure I could find us some leftovers.'

'No, you relax. I'll do it.'

She allowed herself to be dragged into the empty dining-room. James's idea of 'rustling' up dinner was to call Felix and tell him to find them something to eat.

Felix gave *her* a look of hostility, as if it was her fault he was being asked to do a chore so obviously beneath his station. Still, a few minutes later he produced two bowls of steaming chilli, a half-loaf of homemade bread, and two bottles of beer.

Having deposited the fare on the table, his wounded dignity evident in his stiffly upturned nose, Felix slid sulkily away.

The meal looked heavenly to Mandy. She realised she was ravenous.

'What is this?' James asked with distaste.

'Leftover chilli. Wait until you try it. It's divine.' She decided not to tell him about the cigar ash.

'Chilli? I hired a French chef.'

'He didn't even make it to opening day. Why would you hire a French chef for ranch vacations, anyway?' she asked him.

He shrugged. 'That's my personal preference.'

His personal preference. Never mind what was practical or in keeping with the theme of the ranch.

'Mandy, you just don't seem to be yourself,' James commented after a while.

'Don't I?'

'I seem to remember you being very bubbly. Better than Dom Perignon.' He wrinkled his nose charmingly at her.

'It's been a long day,' she said.

'So I heard. Carpenter just accused me of nearly killing you. Is that true?'

'I'm afraid so.'

'No wonder you aren't quite yourself, then!' he said with a laugh.

She stared at him. Could he really not grasp the seriousness of what he'd done?

Maybe it was Brett's fault. Maybe he hadn't communicated it properly. 'What exactly did Brett say to you?'

'He said I stampeded the herd. He told me, in language I won't repeat to a lady, that if I ever brought a helicopter anywhere near his herd again, he'd hang me up on the barn door and let the cowboys throw darts at me.'

Communication didn't come much clearer than that, Mandy thought.

'I thought he overstated his case a bit, but I think he's still miffed about the other thing.'

'You put the lives of people and animals in danger, and you think he overstated the case?' Mandy said, taking a steadying swallow of her beer.

'It's not as if I *meant* to do it, and no one was hurt. What am I supposed to do, wear sackcloth and ashes?'

Brett, she decided, had been in a very bad mood even before he had bumped into her. And who could blame him?

'What "other" thing were you referring to?' she asked.

'Occasionally, I try to broaden the horizons of the ranch a bit. I mean it is *mine*, so why not utilise it?'

'In what way?'

'Well, for instance I got into raising racehorses once. Fabulously exciting having one's own stable, seeing your own silks at the races.'

'What happened?'

'I was the victim of poor management,' James said.

'Brett's?' she asked with astonishment.

'Oh, no. Carpenter runs the ranch, and he does it exceedingly well, but he wouldn't know a thing about dealing with bloodstock. I didn't ask for his input and he didn't offer it.'

'So why did he get "miffed" as you put it, when it didn't work out?'

'He didn't really get miffed about the thoroughbreds. Mildly annoyed, on that one. It was Safariland that miffed him.'

'Safariland?' she echoed.

'I won a pair of giraffes in a poker game. By coincidence, I had just been to a safari park in Southern California that was incredible. I got the idea of doing the same thing here.'

'On the Big Bar L?' she asked with horror.

'Coincidentally, that's exactly what he said, and in that very same tone.'

'What happened?'

'Well, it is *my* ranch so I had the giraffes delivered, but I hadn't taken a few things into consideration. Like the fencing requirements for a giraffe. Or the climate here. I generally only visit in the summer. I guess it's somewhat brutal in the winter months. Much too brutal for a giraffe. Come to think of it, it was rather hard on the thoroughbreds, too.

'Anyway, the upshot is that Brett Carpenter told me to get rid of the giraffes or I'd be looking for a new ranch manager. He didn't say it nearly that civilly, I might add.'

'And you wanted Brett more than the giraffes?'

'Well, it wasn't so much a case of wanting as *needing*. The man is incredible at his job. He has more knowledge about running a ranch in his little finger than I have in my whole head. Than I'd have if I had two heads. He knows it. I know it. There's been some bad years for big beef operations, but he always has this place solidly in the black.'

'But you risked ruffling his feathers by starting the guest-ranch without his approval,' she pointed out.

'We're both still aware that *technically* it is my ranch,' James said with a rueful grin. 'And the whole safari thing was long enough ago that I thought he might have forgotten it by now. Besides, he's not nearly so hostile to the guest-ranch as I thought he'd be.'

'He isn't?' Mandy asked with disbelief.

'He said you and he were out riding today so that he could show you a spot that might be of interest to the guests. That's more participation than I would have ever expected from him.' James twiddled the stem of his glass. 'Or am I mistaken about the direction of his interest?'

'I couldn't tell you the first thing about Brett Carpenter's interests,' she stated uneasily. Then she wondered if she had just missed a chance to level with James about her own feelings.

Level with James about her feelings? She realised she hadn't quite sorted them through herself.

'Ah, well, I seem to have a winning venture on my hands this time, many thanks to you.'

'There really are some difficulties we'll need to talk about before you can even begin to evaluate the success of the guest-ranch operation.'

In the kitchen they heard the smashing of glass. 'Felix, for one,' she said with a sigh.

'Carpenter just gave me an earful about Felix. Could we discuss something else?' he pleaded. 'I just find details so tedious, don't you?'

'It really is kind of important that we get some things sorted out.'

'What's really important is that I'm here, and that I have two weeks to spend with you. What should we do?'

'What should we do?' she echoed.

'Let's fly to Calgary. It's a decent city, you know. Live theatre, sophisticated music, fine dining, dancing. Does any of that appeal to you?'

'Guests are arriving first thing in the morning,' she reminded him.

'Guests, pests,' he said lightly. 'We're going to make the most of our time together.'

'I have a job to do.'

'Well, surely the guests aren't more important to you than me?' he said with surprise.

'James, those people have paid good money to come here, and I can't just abandon them to their own devices.'

'Felix can look after them.'

'Felix can't,' she said.

'Why?'

'Felix is a drunk. That symphony of sound from the kitchen was no doubt the result of his unearthing the cooking sherry.'

'Felix is in the cups again, is he?' James asked with a cheerful lack of concern. 'Maybe, since Carpenter is a little more receptive to this idea——'

'Forget it.'

'Do you have a suggestion, then?'

'I do, actually. I think, for your stay, you should take part in the programme. You'd probably have fun, *and* you could see for yourself what we're doing here.'

'Fun?' he said, with a faint, unpleasant twist to his smile. 'You think I'm going to have fun going on pony rides, learning to barn dance and milking balloons, or whatever it is you do at that silly little rodeo of yours?'

She felt the blood draining from her face. 'If you don't think that sounds fun, what on earth motivated you to start a guest-ranch in the first place?'

'Oh, don't be so serious,' he chided her. 'I see you have a point. I'll participate for as long as I can bear it. But I'm going to steal time alone with you every chance I get. There's nothing wrong with wanting that, is there, Mandy? I've travelled a long way to be with you. Forgive me if I resent sharing you with a bunch of other people.

'Now, the night is young. What do you suggest we do with the rest of it?'

She glanced at her watch. Maybe the night was young for him, but she was going to have to be up at five in the morning to take the bus in to Calgary to meet the guests.

'I'm going to bed,' she told him.

'That sounds delightful,' he said with a wicked grin.

'Alone,' she said firmly.

'Are you the oldest virgin on the face of the earth, or is it just my advances you're immune to?'

'James, I explained to you before that I don't believe in casual sex.'

She thought of the way she had begged Brett to nibble her ears, not a full eight hours ago, and felt a faint flush creep up her cheeks.

James saw the blush and smiled. 'I suppose I'm going to have to marry you, am I?'

'James!' she said, shocked. 'We barely know each other.'

'That's why I'm here. To correct that unfortunate situation. So stay up with me, just for a while, so we can renew our acquaintance . . . and go deeper.'

But with her tummy full of hot chilli, and half a bottle of beer inside her, she could barely keep her eyes open. Besides, she didn't want to encourage James to think their relationship was going to go anywhere. It wasn't. It couldn't.

'I can't. Not tonight.'

'Mandy, whoever would have thought you'd be a party pooper?'

'Yeah,' she said softly. 'Whoever would have guessed that?'

Mandy's alarm worked the following morning, and she accompanied Mick, who drove the bus, into Calgary to pick up passengers from the airport and several Calgary hotels that were prearranged rendezvous points.

'We're missing someone,' she told Mick after the passengers had boarded at the last pick-up point and she had counted heads.

She did a roll call.

Lillian Merriweather was the missing guest.

She sighed. Her fondest hope was that Mrs Merriweather had changed her mind. She wanted to treat that assumption as a fact and head back to the ranch, but she knew if that passenger were anyone other than Brett Carpenter's old flame she would make every effort to clarify what had happened to her.

'I have a phone number here,' she said. 'I'll find a phone booth.' Twenty minutes later she returned to the bus.

'No answer. Mick, we'll have to check each of our rendezvous points again and see if she's there.'

They checked each hotel. Mandy went in and talked to the desk clerks. She tried Mrs Merriweather's phone number again. Finally, knowing she had done all she could do, and knowing she had an obligation to her other guests, she told Mick to start back to the ranch.

No one would ever guess what a deep sense of relief she felt that for some mysterious reason Mrs Merriweather had decided not to have a ranch holiday near her childhood home—and her childhood sweetheart—after all.

Mandy used the time on the bus to break the ice with the guests. She told them the rules, passed out maps of the ranch, and outlined programmes and activities. She also played games and led singalongs.

By the time the passengers had unloaded from the bus, many friendships had already begun, and the guests were ready to have some fun.

She turned them over to Felix and then turned back to Mick, who was unloading suitcases.

'Thank you for being so patient.'

'Aw, weren't nuthin'.' He straightened and looked at her with a grin. 'You were pretty patient the day the bus broke down, too.'

'All I can say is thank goodness you're mechanical.'

'Yeah, it comes in handy all right.' Mick suddenly pushed his cowboy hat up and squinted down the road. 'Well, lookee that.'

Mandy looked.

Mick whistled. 'That's some fancy car. I thought only doctors drove cars like that.'

Or doctor's wives? Mandy thought with sudden insight, as the big white Lincoln Continental glided up beside the bus and stopped beside it.

A smoked window slid silently down.

The woman was beautiful. She had grey eyes, fringed with sooty black lashes. Her hair was ash blonde. Her skin was flawless.

'Good morning,' she said in a husky voice. 'I'm Lillian Merriweather. Is there any place in particular I should park?'

'Right there is fine,' Mandy said, hoping her instant animosity was not too evident.

The purr of the car engine stopped. The woman got out of the car. She was very tall and slender. She was wearing a silk pink Western shirt, tucked into white jeans. On her feet were Western boots of soft cowhide.

She stretched her luscious curves. 'My, I'd forgotten how terrible these roads can be.'

'Actually, we discourage people from bringing their own cars, Mrs Merriweather, for just that reason. But if you did have to drive, it would have been nice if you'd let us know. We spent quite a bit of time today trying to track you down.'

But if the truth were known, Mandy was glad that Lillian Merriweather was rude and inconsiderate. It was able to detract from her perfect looks considerably.

'But I did call!' she said. 'I called last week and said I'd decided to drive.'

And a liar besides, Mandy thought with grim satisfaction.

'I spoke to Fred or Philip. No! Felix. That was it.'

So, she wasn't a rude inconsiderate liar, after all. In fact, Mrs Merriweather was looking at her apologetically. 'I do hope the mix-up didn't cause too much inconvenience. I know several people in this area, and I thought if I had my car I could visit them, time permitting.'

'Welcome to the Big Bar L,' Mandy said, her heart sinking. Lillian Merriweather was a class act. No wonder Brett had been comparing other women to her on and off for so many years.

'Thank you. I've been here many times before. I grew up on the ranch next door.'

'Yes, I know,' Mandy said, and then answered the surprise in Lillian's eyes. 'Brett told me.'

Something softened in those huge grey eyes. 'Then *he* is still here. I wondered.'

Her eyes trailed away from the house and moved towards the corral area.

'If you don't mind, I'd like to have a little stretch after that drive. Maybe I'll go for a little stroll down memory lane.'

'As long as you understand some areas are off limits,' Mandy said a little desperately.

'Off limits?' The woman looked at her with interest.

'The management is quite adamant about guests obeying the posted signs.'

'I understand perfectly,' Lillian said. 'Having grown up on a ranch, I know how dangerous it could be to have greenhorns wandering around at will.' She smiled. 'I suppose I am a greenhorn after all these years. My husband didn't like this country. After my parents sold out there wasn't ever any reason to come back.'

Mandy couldn't help but notice her use of the past tense when she referred to her husband. She had to struggle very hard to fight her nosy instincts.

'My goodness, that's not Brett now, is it?'

Mandy turned her head.

Brett was coming towards them, his jeans faded and tight, his stride long and loose. His shoulders looked so

broad in a dark denim shirt. His cowboy hat, white
today, and immaculately clean, was pulled low over his
eyes. If she was not mistaken, there was a cluster of
prairie wild flowers in one of his hands.

Lillian began to walk towards him, slowly at first, and
then more quickly. She was almost running when she
reached Brett.

He picked her up, right off her elegant feet, hugged
her hard to him, and swung her around.

He set her back down.

Mandy couldn't hear the words they were saying. But
she could see the way they stood so motionless, staring
at each other, drinking each other in.

She saw Brett grin boyishly and hand her the now
crushed flowers. Lillian buried her nose in them.

Mandy was aware they looked good together, because
they were both so tall and slender.

They both seemed to have a certain reserve—a classi-
ness, too.

Mandy turned and bolted up the stairs to the house.

She collided with James in the doorway.

'Mandy——' He looked down at her. 'What happened?' he said, taking her shoulders and looking into
her tear-filled eyes.

'I caught my thumb in the bus door,' she lied.

'Let me kiss it better.'

'No,' she said, jerking away from him.

She realised she had wanted Lillian to be rude and
inconsiderate and a liar, and it was herself that was dem-
onstrating these qualities.

'I'm sorry. I'll just go look after it myself.'

'The guests are getting settled. Will you have a few
minutes to spend with me before you're back on? Maybe

we could go for a walk. I really do want to get to know
you better, Mandy.'

She thought of Brett and Lillian standing in the middle
of that dusty road, entranced with each other.

'Sure,' she said, with a shaky smile. 'Let's go for a
walk. I just have to...uh, run my hand under water. I'll
be right back.'

She dashed up the stairs to her room, closed the door
behind her and burst into tears.

By mid-week she was exhausted. James, true to his
promise, was monopolising every second she wasn't busy
with guests. But it meant too many late nights, too much
energy expended on James that she didn't feel she had
to spare.

On Wednesday she went down to the corrals, feeling
almost as if she was skulking, hiding from James and
his constant demand to be entertained.

The night was blessedly quiet. The stars were winking
out. It felt like she hadn't had a moment to pause since
James had arrived, and she desperately needed this time
to sort through her confusion of feelings.

Lillian, unlike James, was a wonder guest. She made
no demands at all. She seemed content to read, and often
went off to visit old friends. She was quiet and mature,
but also a good sport, which she demonstrated when she
good-naturedly joined in some of the activities.

Mandy could not decipher if the woman had romantic
feelings for Brett or not, though she really couldn't
understand, given their history, how Lillian could *not*
have an attraction to Brett.

She pulled herself up on to the top rail of the fence. The moon was full and she sat in the semi-darkness looking at the dark outline of Tim's filly.

She saw a shape coming down the road, and her impulse was to run. If James had followed her she was going to scream.

Instead, as the form took shape, she felt relief...and dread.

'Hello,' he said, leaning his arms on the top rail of the fence beside her. There was a certain curtness in his greeting.

'Patrolling the grounds?' she asked lightly. 'Am I out of bounds?'

'No. You're not out of bounds.'

'Getting soft?' she queried.

'Probably. Soft in the head.'

Playfully she swiped his cowboy hat, and patted his head.

'Not that I can tell.'

He arrested her hand, his eyes meeting hers with faint warning, and faint question. He took the cowboy hat from her and put it back on his head.

For a moment the silence was tense and electric between them.

'I hear the boss is the life of the party this week.'

She nodded. It was true. Once James had decided to participate, he participated with a vengeance. He was always at the centre of every crowd, always ready to have fun. The guests loved him.

'He likes to have a good time,' she said.

Brett made a sound she couldn't quite interpret.

'You know, there is nothing wrong with having a good time,' she said defensively. She knew that she and James were cut from much the same cloth.

'I never said there was.'

'You have so—just not with words.'

'Look, Mandy, I'm as much for having fun as the next guy—but in proportion to the rest of life. Fun is a part of life—not the purpose of life.'

'Oh, what do you know about the purpose of life?' she said crabbily.

He laughed, a low sound, as velvet as the night. 'Probably nothing. In fact lately, I'd say absolutely nothing. Life has kind of taken me by surprise.'

'In what way?' Her heart was beating in her throat as she looked at his strong profile, silvered by moonlight.

All of her confusion about her feelings suddenly crystallised.

I'm hopelessly in love with this man.

But before he could answer, yet another person came down the road.

'Hello, Lillian,' he said. His voice was without surprise, and Mandy realised they had been planning to meet here.

Hopelessly is right, Mandy thought looking at Lillian. The moonlight did magic things to the other woman's colouring. It also made her look serene and ethereal, like a saint.

'Hello, Brett. And Mandy. Are you going to come with us?'

Lillian was dressed in jeans and a lovely hand knit sweater.

'Come with you?' she echoed.

'Brett and I are going to ride out to the old buffalo jump. We used to always ride at night when the moon was full when we were kids. Have you seen the buffalo jump?'

'As a matter of fact, no,' Mandy said tersely. 'I haven't.' She glared at Brett. He didn't have the imagination that God gave a rock. Was this buffalo jump always where he headed with his dates?

'Would you like to come?' Lillian asked courteously, though Mandy detected no real enthusiasm in the invitation.

'Yes,' she said stubbornly.

'No,' Brett said at the same time.

They stood staring at each other.

Mandy became aware of Lillian's grey eyes moving back and forth between them.

Without another word, she climbed off the fence, turned and walked away from them. Once, he'd told her she was the most beautiful woman he'd ever seen.

Of course, that was back when there had only been one woman in his world. Now there were two. And there was no doubt Lillian was beautiful.

Beautiful, and so much like him in temperament she could have been his sister.

If only she *could* have been his sister.

CHAPTER NINE

'BRETT, do you want to turn around and go back?'

Brett, startled out of his thoughts, gave his attention to Lillian. He was struck anew by how gracefully she was ageing. She was beautiful, strong, mature. And the best rider he'd ever seen, man or woman.

'Go back? Why?'

'You just seem like you aren't enjoying yourself much.'

He could read between the lines. It seemed he wasn't enjoying *her* much.

Chalk another one up to that little green-eyed monster. Here he was being given a second chance with a woman who was suited to him in every way, and he couldn't even enjoy her. That little menace had him so tied up in knots he was barely aware of Lillian, and it had been like that from the day she arrived.

Of course, she'd arrived the day after that idiot young pup who'd inherited this place.

The idiot young pup who'd had the audacity to try and upbraid *him* for the bruises on Mandy's legs.

Brett had let him have it, but in honesty his anger wasn't really at James. It was at the fact he *knew* where those ruddy bruises were. But how the hell could James know? He hadn't said Mandy had told him about them, he'd said he'd *seen* them.

So, not a full half-day since she'd been driving him wild with kisses, another man had been treated to a full view of those lush upper thighs. It pointed in one unavoidable direction.

Brett Carpenter had been played for a fool.

Lillian's arrival had been a relief, a distraction from the painful contractions of his inner turmoil. She'd been a widow for two years, and she was here to see about re-igniting an old flame. She'd made that plain in her wonderful, practical way.

And it had sounded like the best idea he'd heard all summer. Lillian was his type. She came from his world. She'd matured into a woman who was predictable, responsible, reliable . . . and, he'd be willing to bet his last dollar, faithful.

And it certainly didn't hurt that he could see the pain in Mandy's eyes every time Lillian went anywhere near him. There was a juvenile boy on the loose inside him saying, 'Oh, yeah? You want to play hard ball? I can hurt you as good as you hurt me—or better.'

All of which was grossly unfair to the woman riding beside him.

'Why didn't you come home six months ago?' he muttered. Then they could have been safely married— maybe even have had a family on the way—by the time that little green-eyed monster with her stupid socks showed up here.

'What did you say?' Lillian reined in her horse.

He reined in beside her, and they both gazed at the moon.

'I said I wish you would have come back sooner.'

'Brett, did you ever forgive me for marrying Dan Merriweather?'

'That was all a long time ago, Lillian.'

'I said I'd wait, and I didn't.'

'I don't blame you. I had nothing to offer you.'

'You had so much to offer, but I was too young and foolish to see it. To see that it would have been worth the wait.'

'It was a mixed up time for both of us. I couldn't seem to move on from the death of my father.'

'And then I abandoned you, too. I'm sorry. Love must have seemed like a terribly risky business after that. Is that why you never married?'

Was it? 'I don't know,' he said honestly. A few weeks ago he might have thought that was it, exactly. Now, there seemed to be a larger picture.

Big grey eyes latched onto his face, and she leaned closer to him. Her lips touched his.

They were cool and sweet, and fired about as much passion in him as touching his lips to a glass of iced tea.

'It's not going to work, is it, Brett?'

He touched the tear tracking down her beautiful face, and felt to the bottom of his gut what a cad he had been using her to make Mandy jealous, even though it had been almost unconscious.

'No,' he said softly. 'It's not going to work.'

'Does it have something to do with Mandy?' she asked softly.

'I don't know, Lil.' The thoughts had been tormenting him too long, and looking into Lillian's moonbathed sympathetic face, they came spilling out. 'Maybe. She baffles me. She infuriates me. She drives me crazy. And despite all that, I want her. She makes me feel alive. She makes me laugh.'

'I see,' Lillian said calmly. 'So what exactly is it that stops you from telling her how you feel?'

'Shoot. She probably hears it ten times a day. From what I can see she has the same effect on every man she meets.'

'She certainly does have an abundance of effervescent charm. James Snow-Pollington seems quite taken with her.'

'So I've noticed.'

'Do you think she cares for you at all, in a deeper sense?'

He thought of those bruises on her legs. 'I thought she did. Now I don't know. I don't know what goes on inside that little red head at all.'

Without consulting him, Lillian had turned her horse back to the ranch. He didn't argue.

'She and James seem very well suited in some ways,' Lillian said carefully. Despite her care, the dagger-edge still sliced his heart.

'What do you mean?' he asked tersely.

'Temperamentally, they seem to be quite a bit alike. They're both very bubbly, very social, very activity-oriented.'

'That's true,' he bit out.

'How would a girl like that survive out here, Brett?'

'I don't know.'

'I think she'd be bored. I think she'd want you to entertain her.'

He knew exactly how he'd like to entertain a bored Mandy Marlowe. By throwing her across his big brass bed.

'That's not enough,' Lillian said.

'What?'

She smiled knowingly. '*That*.'

'I know.'

'Two people, who find each other attractive and who share the same temperament, and a great deal of common ground—now that's enough.'

But it wasn't. Not any more. Not after having had the sweet thrill of something more. That elusive something that made a man's heart beat faster, and that muddled his thoughts beyond reason. That elusive something, that awareness, that lived in him every second of every day and deep into the night as well.

But even that was not enough if her feelings were not exclusively for him. He'd been surprised to learn how tolerant he could be. But he was a one-woman man, and he needed someone who shared the same values as him. Not someone who kissed one man in the morning and was sharing champagne with another by evening.

'If that scowl gets any worse, you'll be playing the grinch in the Christmas play,' Lillian teased.

'Race you back to the corral,' he challenged.

Lillian won hands down. She was already taking the tack off the horse when he pulled in.

They rubbed down the animals in companionable silence, put the equipment away.

'Would you like a coffee or cookies or something?' Lillian asked.

'No, thanks, not tonight.'

She stood looking at him for a long time. 'If things didn't work out between you and—well, do you think then, you and I might have a chance?'

His life seemed so lonely now. It never had before Mandy, but now it felt like there was a great aching loneliness in him that never went away.

The idea of spending the rest of his days alone in his house, alone at his dinner-table, alone in his bed, had no more appeal.

If it couldn't be Mandy, could it be Lillian? There were so many things he liked about her. Her quietness, her stability, her maturity. She was, without a doubt, beautiful. In so many ways she would be better than emptiness.

'I don't know what to say,' he admitted softly.

She smiled, her heartache showing around the corners of her mouth, and in her eyes. 'You don't have to say anything right now. I don't need an answer right away. Just think about it.'

'All right.'

'Brett? Could you just hold me? Just for a minute?'

He gathered her against his chest, and held her tight. He felt a nice brotherly sensation of caring deeply about her. It was a feeling he was fairly certain no woman would appreciate from a man she had just proclaimed herself to.

Finally, she pulled away. She tucked a wayward strand of that neat hair behind her ear. 'Well, goodnight, Brett.' She turned and walked quickly up the lane towards the big house.

If he was not mistaken he could hear faintly muffled sobs.

Only a month ago, his life had been so blessedly uncomplicated.

No matter what happened, he was not certain he could ever find full contentment in that sweetly uncomplicated lifestyle again.

*   *   *

'Mandy, stop,' James begged. 'Stop it. You are making my sides hurt from laughing.'

She, James, and some of the other guests were practising events for this week's wind-up rodeo, now only two days away.

'OK,' she called, sliding off the bucking barrel the cowboys had rigged up for her. 'That's enough for today. See you all at lunch.'

'I'll help you put the equipment away.'

'Oh, that's all right, James, I can manage.'

'Would you get it through your head that I like being with you?' He gave her a playful little peck on the nose.

She pulled away from him, and he frowned.

'Mandy, don't you like me any more?'

'Of course I like you,' she said.

'I can't believe how much fun I have around you,' James told her. 'I wouldn't have believed it was possible to have this kind of fun way out here in the middle of nowhere.'

She bit her lip. 'Then why did you start a guest-ranch, if you really didn't believe ranches are fun?'

'You keep asking me that.'

'You keep not answering.'

'OK, Mandy, do you want the truth?' He stopped, folded his arms over his chest and looked at her.

'Yes, I do.'

'Fine. I started the guest-ranch so that I would need an activities co-ordinator and I could hire you.'

She stared at him. 'What?'

'I wanted to spend some time with you. I didn't think you would ever agree to go on a vacation with me or anything like that because you're so sweetly old-fashioned.'

'James, that seems like a ridiculous length to go to get to know a girl a little better.'

'Maybe for any other girl it would have been,' he said softly. 'Not for you. And I don't feel its given me an opportunity to know you just a little better. I know you a lot better.'

'Let's go get lunch,' she said brightly.

'Mandy, I need to tell you something. I need to show you something. I need to ask you something.'

'Aren't you just starving?'

'Yes,' he said, taking her wrists and pulling her towards him. 'Starving for this,' he kissed her lips, 'and this,' he kissed her ears, 'and this.' He kissed her neck.

'James! Stop it!'

'Let me have my say,' he said, holding tight still to her wrists. 'I love you. You stole my heart from the first moment that you called me Lord Snow-Pea. Do you remember that?'

'Yes, but——'

He let go of one of her hands and fished in his pocket. 'I've been waiting for the right moment, the right mood, the right time. I guess no time is going to be exactly right. Here.'

She felt herself start to cringe away from the ring box he held out. She wanted to turn and run. She looked at his face, so full of boyish hope. He actually looked shy and scared, not at all worldly and sophisticated.

She took the box, and opened it. She gasped at the brilliantly blinking diamond ring that lay within a bed of black velvet.

'Do you like it?'

She glanced back at him, dumbfounded.

'Will you marry me, Mandy Marlowe?'

Her mouth worked, but no sound came out. His face was so anxious, his normal supreme confidence gone.

'James,' she said gently, 'I'm so honoured that you feel this way for me, but——'

'I know,' he said hastily. 'It's very soon. I've popped this on you very suddenly.'

'Yes,' she agreed.

'Don't give me an answer right away. Think about it.' He laughed nervously. 'I bought the ring quite a while ago—and then found myself staying away from here, because I knew if I saw you again I'd have to ask. And I thought you might say no.'

From a distance she heard the distinctive tinkle of Lillian's laughter.

She looked down at the ring, and felt tears gather in her eyes.

Why not marry James? After all, they had so much in common. They were alike in their temperament and their interests. Wouldn't that have a far better chance of succeeding than following her heart after someone like Brett?

Brett, who was as different from her as night from day?

Brett, the silent, stern cowboy who had somehow made off with her heart.

Would it be fair to James to marry him when she loved another?

She heard the tinkle of that laughter again. Brett seemed to be pursuing his high school sweetheart with all his might.

And really, why not? She could not think of a couple so well suited for each other as Brett and Lillian.

Unless it was herself and James.

Why couldn't James have asked her this six months ago? When having some things in common would have seemed like enough?

Before her heart had known what it was to yearn and burn with an all-consuming fire? Before she had known the exhilaration and the pain of loving someone.

Brett made her mad. He baffled her. She didn't always understand him. But she respected him, and admired him and saw how good he was underneath that stern exterior. Besides, when she was around Brett Carpenter she was one hundred per cent alive.

'Do you want to try on the ring?' James asked eagerly.

No, it would not be fair to marry James when she loved another. But thank goodness he didn't want an answer right away. She needed to think how to put it gently, how to hurt him as little as possible.

She closed the lid on the box, and passed it back to him. 'No. I won't try it on.' There. That was a hint. He could start preparing himself, too.

Except he didn't seem to take it as a hint.

'Shall we go for lunch, then?'

Her ravenous appetite of moments ago was gone.

Funny that Brett, unpretentious cowboy, should be her Prince Charming, and James, rich, titled and charming, was not. Life was full of these grim little ironies.

That night there was a soft knock at Mandy's door.

'Come in,' she called, and nearly died of relief when it was Lillian, and not James.

'Can I talk to you for a minute?'

'Oh, sure.' Mandy cleared some papers off her bed, but Lillian paced over to the window. 'Honestly, Lillian, you are just about the most gorgeous woman I have ever seen. I'd kill for your hair.'

Lillian turned and smiled at her. 'You know, Mandy, I don't think it would be possible to dislike you. Even if a person tried, I just don't see how they could succeed.'

She could tell Lillian someone who had succeeded.

Lillian came and sat on the bed, and gazed at her, one elegant leg folded up under her.

'I'm going to leave tomorrow.'

'But why?'

'I have some urgent things that need looking after in the city.'

Mandy knew she should try and talk her into staying, but in her heart a little bird of hope was fluttering to life. Did this mean nothing had developed between Brett and Lillian?

'He doesn't love me,' Lillian said, with a soft, sad smile.

'I'm sorry,' Mandy said.

'Are you?'

Mandy looked away from that penetrating gaze.

'He doesn't love me,' Lillian repeated, 'but love isn't everything. At a certain age you come to realise love is something of an illusion. It burns so red hot it can burn itself right out. Especially if there's nothing else there. No common ground. No understanding of one another's lifestyles.

'Mandy, can you even imagine what winter is like out here? The wind howls and the snow blows blindingly across the land. Sometimes it's so cold the cattle freeze. It's a lifestyle for women who like to can fruit and cook pies, and sit in front of the fire with a good book. Or for a woman who is hardy enough to be at her husband's side through thick and thin.

'It's a lifestyle for a woman who doesn't mind being alone, and who doesn't need to have things happening at breakneck speed around her. For a woman who knows how dangerous and lonely this work can be for her man, and who can accept things going from calm to crisis in the blink of an eye.'

'Why are you telling me this?' Mandy asked.

'Because I don't think you're that kind of woman. I like you. As I said earlier, I think it would be impossible not to. But do I think you could last a winter out here? No. Do I think you could adapt to this lifestyle? No.'

'I still don't understand why you're telling me this,' Mandy said stiffly.

'I've seen the light in your eyes when you look at him, Mandy.'

'You have?' Mandy asked despondently.

Lillian nodded. 'I have.'

'Don't you see it doesn't matter how much light I have in my eyes?' Mandy said, trying for a light tone, and failing. 'He's got to feel something, too.'

'Mandy, I don't mean any offence, but you're kind of like an earthquake. A whirlwind. I think you could knock a man off balance and walk away with his heart and soul before he even knew what hit him.'

'I could?' Mandy said eagerly.

'I'm not sure I meant it as a compliment,' Lillian responded softly.

'What are you saying?'

Lillian sighed. 'James loves you, doesn't he?'

'He thinks he does.'

'I'm saying if you have a choice to make, choose James. That must seem very personal and interfering of me, but as an outsider looking in, and as a woman with a bit more experience than you, it is so obvious that choice would make you happiest in the long run.'

Lillian reached out and squeezed her hand. 'I believe that with all my heart.'

'Blair, do you think I've gotten good enough to take a horse out by myself for awhile?'

Ever since that humiliating experience with Brett, Mandy had been at the corrals every spare minute getting Blair to help her with her riding.

'Sure you have, Mandy. Clara's all saddled. Take her.'

Mandy mounted the quiet little mare and headed out into the grasslands. She sat the horse with far more ease than she had just a few days ago. She controlled her easily, even though, to be certain she was no great challenge to control.

She rode to a high point in the land and stopped. Her breath caught in her throat. The land rolled on endlessly to the east, and to the west the Rocky Mountains jutted up, harshly beautiful against a blue Alberta sky.

The wind was blowing and it tangled in her hair and touched her face.

The scent of the horse was tangy and mingled with the scent of dry grass under a hot summer sun.

She remembered first arriving here and thinking this landscape so unbearably bleak. But now it tugged at some place inside her.

She got off the horse, and stood, eyes closed, holding her face to the light, and feeling the warmth pour into her.

A sound startled her. She opened her eyes. The heat shimmered off the land in waves. In the distance it looked as if a wagon train was moving towards her. Surely it was just the billowing white clouds?

She squinted. It still looked like wagons rolling steadily across an endless land.

Suddenly, within her, was a deep feeling of connection. A deep sense of kinship with the women who had ridden those wagons across this land that must have seemed so frightening and empty to them. Ridden those wagons towards a future that was a great unknown.

Still, they had come. Why?

She felt it. Singing in the wind all around her. Love. And the courage born of love. The faith that where love went good things would follow. Certainty that love was the most powerful force in the universe—more powerful than this great emptiness, more powerful than winters so cold cattle would freeze, more powerful than all the obstacles man and nature could put before it.

The wagon train was gone. Only the shimmering heat-waves remained. It had been a mirage. The song of the wind stilled. All that remained was a great silence.

But in that great silence, she found her answer. In the sudden peace that unravelled in her belly, she knew that answer was the right one.

She rode back to the ranch. She took the saddle off Clara, took care of her feet, and brushed her. The small routines felt good. They made her feel strong and capable.

When she could linger no longer, she went in search of James.

She found him lounging by the pool, a housecoat wrapped around himself.

'Confounded wind,' he said to her. 'A man could freeze to death after going for a swim. In July.'

But she felt as if she had heard the wind sing its song. For her, it would never be 'that confounded wind' again.

She went and sat down on the bottom of his lawn chair.

'James, I've been doing a great deal of thinking.'

'I thought so.'

'I care about you deeply. You have been a wonderful friend to me. You have incredible enthusiasm for life, and for laughter.'

'A poetic brush-off?' James said, but his voice did not echo the humour of the words.

'I can't marry you, James.'

'Naturally, that's not what I had hoped your answer would be.'

'I'm sorry.'

'Me, too. It would seem I've made something of a fool of myself.' He gave her a gentle shove, and she stood up. He did too, pulling the housecoat tight around himself.

'I don't think you're a fool, James.'

'No? Would you like to see the bill for this little failed romance?'

'What do you mean?'

'The guest-ranch is a flop, Mandy. Only about half the guests were paying concerns. I subsidised it because . . . well, just because.'

'James, didn't you know I would have been just as happy with pizza and a movie?'

'I do seem to have a weakness for the grand gesture,' he said with forced lightness.

'You don't have to pretend it doesn't hurt.'

'Really?' he said, and his lip curled up. 'Thank goodness. In that case, you're fired. As of next week there is no more Big Bar L guest-ranch.'

She stared at him. 'James, you can't do that. People have booked holidays right up until the end of the summer.'

'You know something?' I can do anything I want. That's something you and Carpenter both need to learn.'

He wasn't hiding any of his feelings now. Anger was rolling off of him in ugly waves.

'If I ever find out that he had anything to do with your not agreeing to marry me, I'll fire him faster than he can ride a cow horse around a barrel.'

'James! What would make you say such a thing?'

'I've seen the way you look at him.'

She could hardly deny she looked at him, especially since this was the second person in less than twenty-four hours to comment on *how* she looked at him.

Suddenly the anger was gone, and James just stood there looking sad and defeated.

'Mandy,' he said softly. 'I think you're making a mistake not to marry me. But I think it would be an even bigger one to think you could ever adjust to life out here.'

'Luckily,' she said with a toss of her head, 'I haven't been asked.'

'Yeah,' he murmured, and she heard a trace of that vindictiveness back in his voice. 'Luckily you haven't.'

CHAPTER TEN

THE bus pulled up in front of the big house for the last time. Mandy watched from the porch swing. When these guests left, there would be no more guests.

Her own little car was packed and waiting. She would just say goodbye.

'Hello, Mandy.'

She swivelled her head. 'Brett,' she said coolly. She looked away swiftly. She felt too vulnerable to Brett. She did not want him to know what she was thinking and feeling right now. She did not want him to guess that her inner landscape was, at this moment, big, and lonely and bleak.

He walked right back into her range of vision. He had taken off his hat and was turning it again and again in his fingers. It was his white hat today, not his working hat. His jeans were pressed and his boots shiny. A special occasion, saying goodbye.

'I came to say goodbye to Tim.'

'He's in the house.'

He took a deep breath. 'I came to say goodbye to you, too,' he said softly.

'All right. Goodbye.'

'Mandy, I'm sorry.'

'I'm the one who uses apologies inappropriately, remember?'

'I am sorry.'

'Why? Is it your fault?'

171

'No, but——'

'Brett, just leave it alone. You knew this moment was coming from the day the ranch opened its doors to guests. You knew James wasn't serious about the idea. You were right. You were perfectly justified in viewing me with contempt. Now go gloat by yourself somewhere.'

'I'm not gloating, Mandy, and as for viewing you with contempt, nothing could be further from the truth.'

She looked at his face. He looked tired and sad, not like a man who was gloating at all. She looked swiftly away from him. The knowledge that she was never going to see him swirled inside her like a black cloud.

'I came to really respect how you did your job, Mandy.'

'Thank you,' she said stiffly.

He looked as if he had more to say. His weight shifted uncomfortably from one booted foot to the other.

'Mandy, is there anything I can do to help?'

'You didn't want to help keep the guest-ranch going. I won't give you the pleasure of helping shut it down.'

'I'm not exactly dancing, Mandy.'

'Well, maybe later,' she said with a shrug.

Strong hands clamped on her elbows and she found herself lifted out of the seat, being forced to stare into furious green eyes.

Her resolve faded. Her resolve to leave here without endangering his job, not to mention with her dignity intact.

He was standing too close. He smelled of soap and spice and sunshine. Behind the anger in his eyes was some unfathomable hurt.

She reached up and touched his rough-whiskered cheek. His hand closed over hers, and moved the fingers to his mouth. He kissed them tenderly.

That feeling she had had before while riding came upon her. Stronger this time: that she rode where others had gone before her. That the strength of the land was surrounding her and soothing her, that the song of the wind was hers alone.

If you love something, Brett had said once, you don't ever lose it. Was that true? Would the spirit of her love for Brett keep her warm through the long nights of the approaching seasons?

She never knew what startled the calm, little mare. Only that one moment she was riding along, feeling peaceful, strangely at one with herself and the universe, strangely trusting of the process of life, when the little mare exploded under her like a powder keg.

Mandy grabbed wildly for the saddle horn, then realised with terror that the whole saddle was sliding. She fell, but her foot was hooked in the stirrup. The panicked horse dragged her. She felt her head smash against a rock, and then mercifully, her foot yanked free of the stirrup.

She gasped for breath, and stared at the sky. She felt like she was looking at it through a tunnel, the bright blue sky shining like a beacon at the end of darkness. But the blue was shrinking and the black was growing. Finally the blue was just a pinprick of light in the darkness, and then there was nothing.

Brett put Tim's filly on the long lunge, uncaring that he wasn't exactly dressed for work. He cracked the whip. He needed to focus on anything but Mandy, anything but the distance in those green eyes when she had looked at him. No, *through* him.

He had watched her from the shadows as she had hauled her suitcase to her car. He had wanted to go and help her, but he couldn't. He couldn't help her leave him. He couldn't even watch her go. He had turned swiftly away and come here as soon as he had heard the car start. Until that very second, there had been a funny little maybe refusing to die in his soul. But at the sound of her car starting that last spark had sputtered and died.

Even though he knew Lillian had been right.

He had to let her go. This life, this land had nothing to offer a woman like Mandy. In that last meeting, he had hoped she would do or say something that would blow every rational thought out of his head.

It had almost happened, too.

Almost.

He had almost begged her to stay, to see what they could do with the power of love, to see if love would be enough, more than enough to help them over life's obstacles.

But he hadn't. Some might say he was a chicken, but he knew it had taken more strength than he'd known he had not to beg her, to respect that her feelings did not reflect his.

Oh, she'd touched him, to be sure, and when she had touched him that electrical link had surged through them and bonded them together, as it always did. But that was something else Lillian had been right about. That wouldn't be enough.

She had to love him as much as he loved her. She had to love just him, for the rest of her life. How could she? How could she do that when every man who ever met her fell just as hard and just as fast as he himself had?

With a sigh, he stopped the filly and went and took the lead off. It wasn't working. It wasn't taking his mind off a bloody thing.

What would work? Shutting down the pool? No, ghosts of her would linger at the pool. Ghosts of her would linger everywhere. Even his own bedroom was not safe from her memories.

How long did it hurt like this, anyway?

He coiled the rope and went to put it away. The far-off thud of galloping hooves turned his head.

He moved to where his view of the road coming into the corrals was better. He squinted, and his heart stopped for a full beat.

A horse was charging towards him, the saddle slipped right over on to the horse's side. No rider.

He forced himself to be calm as the horse galloped in and then stood, panting and shaking, frothing sweat. Who had been out? The horse wasn't one that any of his cowhands favoured, he could tell that at a glance. The saddle did not belong to any of his men, either.

The horse was one of the horses used for guest trail-rides. But the guests were all gone.

Blair? Blair would never put a saddle on so badly that it would slip like this.

Mandy. It was as if her perfume filled his mind. But of course it wasn't Mandy. He'd seen her drive away.

No, that wasn't precisely what he'd seen, he reminded himself. To assume Mandy would follow anything through to its natural conclusion was probably a wrong assumption.

There was an old bell on the side of the barn that they rang only in emergencies. His heart beating hard, he went over and rang it. Someone was missing off that horse.

And he'd be willing to bet whoever had come out of that saddle was hurt.

Cowboys were coming from all directions—and coming fast. That bell probably hadn't been used in more than a year. Even James was familiar with what the bell meant and was running down the lane from the big house.

'Did anybody see who left on this horse?' Brett asked first.

They shook their heads.

James arrived, panting.

Brett asked the question he didn't want the answer for.

'Is Mandy's car still in the parking lot?'

'Yes, I walked right by it. I noticed she had a teddy-bear belted into the front seat.'

An empty car would have been frightening enough. It meant it could be her. It meant it probably was her. But there was something about that teddy-bear in the front seat that brought her warmth and her laughter right into the centre of that grim circle of men. An ominous silence crept over them. And in the face of each man looking at him for guidance, Brett saw the devotion they felt for her. Each of these men, even James, had had the courage to love her, to freely let his love for her show. It was showing in their faces now.

Suddenly he understood what he had not seen before. Mandy belonged here.

She had been brought to this lonely place to bring them her gifts. Her laughter, her irrepressible enthusiasm, and her love.

And everyone who met her had accepted her gifts, and loved her as she deserved to be loved. Everyone except him.

Who needed her gifts most of all.

There was a fearful anguish in him that threatened to paralyse him. But he couldn't allow that to happen. 'Burt, get me a map.'

'Yessir.'

Sickly, he wondered if he would ever have a chance to tell her that. That you belonged wherever people gave their hearts to you.

But he couldn't afford to be sentimental right now. The map arrived, and they all bent around it.

'Bud, you and Mick do this section to the west. Bring rifles. If you find her, fire a three shots. Don't miss an inch of ground.'

'We won't miss an inch, boss.'

One by one, he assigned men places in the search. But they knew and he knew how big this country was. And how small she was.

Finally, everybody was ready to go or gone. Someone had saddled his horse for him, and he felt grateful. He would ride alone, scanning the area that led to the cottonwoods.

James stood there, among the settling dust, looking very alone.

'As soon as that helicopter comes, get him to start here,' Brett said pointing at the map, 'and sweep out this way.'

'Yes, I've got it. Carpenter—er—Brett——'

Brett curbed his impatience to be gone. 'Yeah?'

'I think this may be my fault.'

'It's nobody's fault.' He slipped a rifle into the sheath on his saddle.

'I asked her to marry me, you know.'

Dammit, didn't the man know every second counted? Brett untied his horse and leapt into the saddle.

'She said no.'

'That's tough,' Brett said wheeling his horse away. Somewhere in his heart bells sounded in jubilation that she had said no, but there was no time for that now.

'She said no because she's in love with you.'

Brett wheeled back and rode very close to James. 'Did she say that to you?'

'No. And, to my deep shame, I told her if she said it to you, I'd fire you. I think she was feeling terrible pressure. I think it's my fault she did this, took that horse when she barely knows how to ride——'

Brett took a deep and steadying breath. What he wanted to say was that he was going to hog-tie James and drag him behind his horse until they found Mandy.

But he looked at him. He was a man in pain, that was all. And if anybody could empathise with a man in Mandy Marlowe pain it was him.

He reached down and gave James's shoulder a swift, hard squeeze. 'I'll find her.'

He saw her from a long way off. She was wandering drunkenly in absolutely the wrong direction. Her knees folded under her, and she fell and lay there, from the distance looking like a small bundle of colourful rags.

He spurred his horse towards her, vaulted from the saddle, and went to her. He crouched beside her, rolled her tenderly over, bit his lip at the dried blood that had dripped down her face. Her chest was rising and falling steadily, and she looked as peaceful as she had that day he had burst into her bedroom. He wanted to just hold her, but he forced himself to check her carefully for broken bones.

Satisfied, he gently gathered her to him, and held her. She weighed about as much as a feather. He kissed her cheek and was rewarded when her eyes opened.

She gave him a sleepy smile. 'Heaven?'

'What, little darlin'?'

'Died,' she muttered. 'Heaven.'

'No, you're not dead.'

'Knew it. Couldn't have you this life but love won't be thwarted.' Each word was said so thickly and slowly, with such fierce concentration.

'You're not dead, silly,' he said with tender exasperation. 'You can have me this life. Every day for whatever we've got left of it. Think you can stand that?'

She looked at him with puzzlement. 'Brett?'

He sighed. She didn't even know who she was talking to. 'Yeah, it's me.'

'My head hurts. Really hurts.'

'OK, OK, love. I'll look after you.' Right now, though, he needed to let the others know he'd found her.

She held to him with surprising strength. 'Don't let me go, Brett, don't ever let me go.'

'I won't,' he assured her. Her eyes closed.

It was a promise he knew he had to break. He went to his saddle and got the rifle. He fired it three times in the air.

He got his canteen and put water on a cloth. He touched it to her dry lips and mopped some of the blood off her.

'Don't let me go,' he whispered when he had done all he could do. He pulled her limp form back into the circle of his arms. 'Don't ever let me go.'

Minutes later the helicopter was roaring over them. It landed and James got out. Brett settled her in there as well as he could. He stood back, feeling his heart was breaking.

'You go with her. The pilot will take you straight to the hospital in Calgary,' James yelled. 'I'll look after getting your horse back to the ranch.'

Brett stared at his boss in amazement, and then a slow smile spread across his face. For the first time, he was seeing some evidence that when James grew up he was going to be a fine man. He gave him a quick closed-fist tap on the shoulder, and got in the helicopter with Mandy.

Flowers. There were flowers everywhere. Yellows and reds and every shade of the rainbow.

'Mandy?'

She turned her head painfully, and the tears stung at her eyes. 'Brett,' she whispered. She studied him. His face was grey with exhaustion.

He reached out and took her hand.

'I fell off the horse, didn't I?'

'It looked as if the saddle slid.'

'I probably didn't do it up right. A regular dude. Oh well, no more dudes for you.'

'Well, that's not precisely right.'

'Has James reconsidered the guest-ranch?'

'God forbid!'

'Where are we?'

'At the Foothills Hospital in Calgary.'

'I thought maybe I was in your bed,' she said with thick disappointment. 'I guess I need an invitation.'

He smiled at her, smoothed her hair back from her brow. 'Consider yourself invited.'

'I always hoped . . . maybe . . . you'd invite me back.'

'Really? Let me look at your eyes. Good. Your pupils are still dilating evenly.'

'Rats. I thought you wanted to look *into* my eyes, not at them.'

'Another time,' he assured her.

'Why are you here?'

'Because I promised you I wouldn't leave you.'

'You're an honourable man,' she whispered, her eyes shutting.

'Mandy?'

'Um?'

'Because I love you. That's why I'm here.'

She muttered something. He was not quite sure, but he thought she said, 'Heaven.'

When she woke again there seemed to be even more flowers. Brett was gone.

Of course he was gone, she thought. He'd probably never even been here. Her mind had been playing some wild tricks on her. That hit on the head had conked her 'wishful' button, because her mind wanted to think Brett had found her and held her and told her delicious things about loving her and spending their lives together. Her mind wanted her to believe that Brett had sat in this chair, and told her he loved her.

This of course was the same mind that had told her firmly that the nurse assisting in the emergency room was her Aunt Polly, who had been dead for fifteen years.

She sat up slowly, and painfully. Feeling like an eighty-year-old woman, she went to the bathroom, then shuffled back and looked at the cards on the flowers.

James. Bud. Mick. Burt. Tim. Charity and Matthew. Guests from the summer. Staff from her school in Vernon. Staff from Anpetuwi. Even Felix had sent her a bouquet.

There was love all around her. Why did she feel so empty, craving a love she could not have?

'You get back into bed this minute, or you'll have me to deal with.'

She turned slowly.

Brett stood in the doorway, hatless for once, his hair black and shiny and curly. He looked so wonderfully familiar. His face was whisker-roughened, and she remembered how those whiskers felt scraping against her cheek. She smiled when she noticed he was wearing a green scrub shirt instead of one of his usual ones.

'Brett——'

'Get into that bed.'

'Why are you wearing——?'

'Now!'

She slipped into bed. 'So, are you going to become a surgeon now?'

He glanced down at the shirt as if it irritated him that it had attracted her attention. 'One of the nurses gave it to me. I think she was trying to tell me I don't smell so good.'

'How long have you been here?'

'Three days.' He moved over to the bed.

'You smell heavenly.' The words came out of her before she could stop them. She felt colour creep up her face. 'Why? Why are you here?'

'Because I'm an honourable man,' he told her with a tired lop-sided grin. He sank down on the edge of the bed, and took her hand between his.

Honour. It was not the answer she might have hoped for. His hand was strong and hard around hers.

'Aren't the flowers beautiful?' she said, feeling suddenly shy of his closeness, uncertain what she should say or do, certain only that she wouldn't let go of his hand unless he snatched it away.

'Beautiful,' he said, his eyes locked on her face.

She blushed harder. 'Imagine Tim spending his hardearned money on flowers for me. He wouldn't have done that four weeks ago.'

'I told him he could stay the rest of the summer despite the guest-ranch closing down. Did you know that?'

'No. I didn't.'

'You know what he said?'

She shook her head. 'What did he say?'

'He said his mother needed him. He said when his dad died it made him afraid of being loved, afraid of loving. He wanted everybody to hate him instead of love him. He thought that would be easier.'

'Oh, Brett.'

'He taught me something. You see, I wanted to take the easy way, too. All my life, I've been a loner. My dad died when I was a young man. Maybe, right then, I made a decision just like Tim's. That it would be easier to be lonely. Love is so full of pitfalls. It's unpredictable. It's not easily tamed or controlled.'

'You're right,' she agreed sadly. 'You're absolutely right.'

'And I don't think anybody has ever successfully figured out why some relationships work and some don't.

I mean, I've heard people say of a couple, "Oh, they'll never make it, they're too different." But sometimes they do.'

'That's right,' Mandy agreed, 'and sometimes it's the ones that you think are perfect for each other that just don't have what it takes.'

'Mandy, I don't think we're perfect for each other. You're a city girl and I'm a country boy. You take life too lightly and I take it too seriously.'

'I never said I was the perfect match for you!' she sputtered indignantly.

'You like to argue all the time, and I'm a peace-loving man.'

'I am not argumentative!' She snatched her hand away from him.

'You like action and I like quiet.'

'A flower vase over your head is the action I'd most like to see right now.'

'And, besides that, you're way too short for me.'

'For you? I wouldn't have you if you were——'

'And I've always been wary of redheads. Violent,' he said, gently removing the flower vase from her hands.

She folded her arms over her chest and glared at him.

'And not one of those differences has stopped me,' he said quietly. 'Not one of them has stopped me from falling head over heels in love with you.'

Her mouth dropped open.

'My intellect kept telling me, "She's not the girl for you. She's outrageous, impulsive, irrepressible." And my heart kept saying, "maybe that's just what you need, you sober-sided old goat."

'Mandy, I don't want my life back the way it was before you. It's as if you lit it up with colour when everything had been grey; it's as if you breathed laughter into a place where laughter hadn't been for a long time.

'This is the craziest thing I've ever done, but Mandy Marlowe, would you be my wife?'

'I don't know, Brett.' She studied his features with frank adoration. 'You're awfully tall for me. You're sense of humour is underdeveloped and your sense of adventure needs a good deal of work.'

'Just answer yes or no,' he said grimly.

'Don't be so bossy. You live in the middle of no-where——'

'Mandy!'

'You could never call me green-eyed monster again, of course...'

'I'm going to put my hands on either side of your neck now,' he said drily. 'I'll stop squeezing when you give me your answer. But only if it's the right one.'

'Brett, you are absolutely the wrong man for me. I've known that from the start. But I love you.' All the teasing was gone from her voice. 'I love you without reason and beyond thought. I love you with my whole heart and my whole soul.

'I don't know what tomorrow holds, but I know if it doesn't hold you, it doesn't seem very inviting.

'Yes. I'll marry you. I'll have your children. I'll learn to ride horses and can peaches.' She frowned. 'But I should warn you that marrying me might have a higher price than you anticipated.'

She told him about James's suspicion of her strong feelings towards Brett, about his threat to fire him.

'I'll just drag him behind my horse until he comes around,' Brett said with a twinkle in his eye.

'Be serious!'

'I thought you were going to teach me not to be so serious. I'm practising.'

'You've already talked to James,' she deduced.

'That's right. He's wished us the best.'

'Wished us the best? How did he know I would say yes?'

'I knew myself, actually, before you answered.'

'You did? How?'

'This light came on in your eyes. This incredible brilliant light that told me you planned to love me forever, and that you had planned to do that even if I let you go.'

'You're right.'

'I know.'

'Come here,' she whispered, shifting over.

He climbed on the narrow bed beside her. 'I planned to love you forever, too. Even if I was fool enough to let you go.'

'Brett, what if I hadn't fallen off that horse? What if I had got in my car and driven away?'

'I think in a week or two the pain would have been unbearable and I would have come after you. I don't think I would have been able to bear the emptiness of that ranch without you on it.'

'I guess I saved you the trouble.'

'You have a troubling way of saving someone trouble,' he pointed out.

'Once you told me I was trouble. In capital letters.'

'Well,' he drawled, 'I can't quite take that one back.'

'Try this for trouble,' she murmured, and offered him her lips. He took them with hunger, and with reverence.

'My God, woman, you are red-hot,' he whispered in between kisses.

'Red-hot?' she mumbled back in between her own greedy little kisses. 'Do you mean the kind that burns itself out in one sizzling summer?'

'No, ma'am. I mean the kind that creates a bank of glowing embers that can keep a man warm for a lifetime.'

'Oh,' she murmured huskily. 'Oh!' she said as he nipped at her ears. 'Ouch,' she cried as his ardour deepened. 'Oh, Brett, I'm sorry. My head hurts.'

'You were right. Trouble. Besides, I think we've been here before,' he said drily. 'One of these days, you're going to run out of excuses.'

'If I don't,' she told him shyly, 'I can get married in white.'

For a minute he didn't understand what she was saying, and then he smiled softly. 'You mean with all the men who have fallen in love with you——'

'Really, Brett, you do tend to overestimate my attractiveness to the opposite sex.'

'No, I don't. You mean you're still——?'

'Yes. I've waited all my life for you.'

He gathered her in his arms, being very careful of her head. 'I've waited all my life for you. I can't wait to take you home.'

She sighed with deep contentment. 'I'm in your arms, Brett. We are home. Forever.'

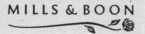

Look out for Temptation's bright, new, stylish covers...

They're Terrifically Tempting!

We're sure you'll love the new raspberry-coloured Temptation books—our brand new look from December.

Temptation romances are still as passionate and fun-loving as ever and they're on sale now!

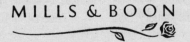

MILLS & BOON

Next Month's Romances

Each month you can choose from a wide variety of romance with Mills & Boon. Below are the new titles to look out for next month, why not ask either Mills & Boon Reader Service or your Newsagent to reserve you a copy of the titles you want to buy – just tick the titles you would like and either post to Reader Service or take it to any Newsagent and ask them to order your books.

Please save me the following titles:

	Please tick	✓
TRIAL BY MARRIAGE	*Lindsay Armstrong*	
ONE FATEFUL SUMMER	*Margaret Way*	
WAR OF LOVE	*Carole Mortimer*	
A SECRET INFATUATION	*Betty Neels*	
ANGELS DO HAVE WINGS	*Helen Brooks*	
MOONSHADOW MAN	*Jessica Hart*	
SWEET DESIRE	*Rosemary Badger*	
NO TIES	*Rosemary Gibson*	
A PHYSICAL AFFAIR	*Lynsey Stevens*	
TRIAL IN THE SUN	*Kay Thorpe*	
IT STARTED WITH A KISS	*Mary Lyons*	
A BURNING PASSION	*Cathy Williams*	
GAMES LOVERS PLAY	*Rosemary Carter*	
HOT NOVEMBER	*Ann Charlton*	
DANGEROUS DISCOVERY	*Laura Martin*	
THE UNEXPECTED LANDLORD	*Leigh Michaels*	

If you would like to order these books in addition to your regular subscription from Mills & Boon Reader Service please send £1.90 per title to: Mills & Boon Reader Service, Freepost, P.O. Box 236, Croydon, Surrey, CR9 9EL, quote your Subscriber No:................................. (if applicable) and complete the name and address details below. Alternatively, these books are available from many local Newsagents including W H Smith, J Menzies, Martins and other paperback stockists from 13 January 1995.

Name:...

Address:..

................................Post Code:........................

To Retailer: If you would like to stock M&B books please contact your regular book/magazine wholesaler for details.

You may be mailed with offers from other reputable companies as a result of this application. If you would rather not take advantage of these opportunities please tick box. ☐